Praise for *Nick & Jake*

"*Nick & Jake* is a feast of a book, packed with subtle flavors and exotic spices to satisfy the palate of the literary and historical gourmet, but just plain delicious for any reader. You don't have to get all the references to join the fun - I'm proud to say I got most of them! - but the more of them you recognize, the more satisfying it is."

—Bill Press, Radio and TV commentator and host, *The Bill Press Show*

"*Nick & Jake* is an hysterical stroll through the Cold War era with many of the most colorful characters of that time. Readers of a certain age will recall with more than a touch of nostalgia a time when personal relations mattered more than institutional ties, and younger readers will conclude that their parents and grandparents may not have been such fuddy-duddies after all. It is a wonderful tale of American expatriates dabbling in big power intrigue without ever forsaking the three martini lunch."

—Joseph C. Wilson, former diplomat and presidential adviser

"What a tour! What a hoot! A visit to the surreality of 1953: from McCarthy and Christine Jorgensen, to Allen Dulles, the Deux Magots Café, Saigon, Iran, Pete Seeger, and Thelonious Monk! This is a hilarious—and frequently painful—visit to the time!"

—Jim Guy Tucker, former governor of Arkansas

"Fitzgerald and Hemingway, hold on to your iconic backsides. Tad and Jonathan Richards have rewritten both you and the mid-twentieth century with now hilarious, now poignant, ever-fascinating effect. History and literature will never be quite the same."

—Roger Morris, former National Security Council staffer, historian, and presidential biographer

"An engaging excursion down the rabbit hole into Literaryland and the Fearful Fifties, to invoke the specters of Allen Dulles, Roy Cohn, Christine Jorgensen, and others of that era in twisted relationships with Nick Carraway and Jake Barnes. Lewis Carroll could have written it, but he may not have been able to handle the sex scenes."

—Pat Oliphant, Pulitzer Prize–winning political cartoonist

"*Nick & Jake* reminds us of history that needs remembering, but sometimes it makes us laugh so hard we almost forget."

—United States Senator Tom Udall

T0109244

"If you were enchanted by Woody Allen's *Midnight in Paris,* you will love immersing yourself in another historical period filled with wit and panache, *Nick & Jake.* The Richards brothers bring their playful creativity and intelligent writing to this treasure of a book."

—Valerie Plame Wilson, former CIA operations officer

"Carraway and Barnes begin as proxies for their creators; their letters recall familiar cadences in Fitzgerald's and Hemingway's prose. It's a great hook, but as the novel spools out and hijinks ensue—political, romantic, sexual—Nick and Jake acquire more distinction. Bidding them good-bye a second time is sweet sorrow indeed. In addition to providing incisive political commentary, resurrecting cultural icons, and breathing life into fictional heroes, the Richards brothers shine a warm, nostalgic light on the lost art of letter writing. *Nick & Jake* approximates the ebb and flow of missives between friends, lovers, even adversaries. Offered here are the rhythms of relationships fostered through the shared mind-space of language, and the sweet anticipation of awaiting a response. *Nick & Jake* proves the epistolary art may yet live."

—Robert Burke Warren, Chronogram.com

NICK & JAKE

NICK & JAKE

An Epistolary Novel

Jonathan Richards
and Tad Richards

ARCADE PUBLISHING • NEW YORK

To Claudia Jessup and Pat Richards.
We couldn't have done this—or anything else,
come to think of it—without you.

Copyright © 2014 by Tad Richards and Jonathan Richards

All rights reserved. No part of this book may be reproduced in any manner without the express written consent of the publisher, except in the case of brief excerpts in critical reviews or articles. All inquiries should be addressed to Arcade Publishing, 307 West 36th Street, 11th Floor, New York, NY 10018.

Arcade Publishing books may be purchased in bulk at special discounts for sales promotion, corporate gifts, fund-raising, or educational purposes. Special editions can also be created to specifications. For details, contact the Special Sales Department, Arcade Publishing, 307 West 36th Street, 11th Floor, New York, NY 10018 or info@skyhorsepublishing.com.

Arcade Publishing® is a registered trademark of Skyhorse Publishing, Inc.®, a Delaware corporation.

Visit our website at www.arcadepub.com.

10 9 8 7 6 5 4 3 2 1

Library of Congress Cataloging-in-Publication Data is available on file.

ISBN: 978-1-62872-320-5

Printed in the United States of America

1953

It was a year unlike any other. On January 20, Gen. Dwight Eisenhower was sworn in as President of the United States in a ceremony broadcast to 21 million black-and-white television sets. The hunt for Reds was in full swing, spearheaded by Joe McCarthy in the U.S. Senate. On Broadway, Arthur Miller attacked the communist witch hunts with *The Crucible*; and in the movies, Elia Kazan was making *On the Waterfront* in defense of naming names. Television newsman Edward R. Murrow began work on an exposé of the tactics of Senator McCarthy.

In June, convicted atomic spies Julius and Ethel Rosenberg died in the electric chair, leaving two orphaned boys. (A half-century later, Soviet documents confirmed Ethel's innocence.) The prosecution had been spearheaded by an ambitious young lawyer named Roy Cohn, who was now Chief Counsel for Senator McCarthy's committee. Cohn and his friend G. David Schine left on a book-banning junket through American government libraries in Europe, to the embarrassment of the American diplomatic corps, and the great entertainment of the European press. When Schine was drafted later that year, Cohn's threats to retaliate by exposing the Army as riddled with Reds eventually led to McCarthy's condemnation by the Senate.

Around the world there was turmoil. America was bogged down in an undeclared war in Korea. In Vietnam, France (with quiet American help) struggled to hold onto the vestiges of its Indochina empire, while back in Paris, governments spun in and out of power through a revolving door. Soviet dictator Joseph Stalin died. America announced it had the H-bomb; a few months later, so did the USSR, and the dance of terror between the two superpowers was joined.

Two of Eisenhower's chief advisers made anti-Communism their personal crusade. John Foster Dulles was named Secretary of State, while across town, his brother Allen was sworn in as the first civilian director of the fledgling Central Intelligence Agency. While Foster articulated the Domino Theory, Allen's CIA would undertake spying on Americans, mind-control experiments, assassinations, and coups. Among its accomplishments was the subsidizing of cultural organizations, including the creation of the international leftist journal *Encounter*, edited by a former City College Trotskyite named Irving Kristol (later a founder of neoconservatism) and British poet Stephen Spender. More significant, the CIA instituted a policy of nation-building, orchestrating the overthrow of the democratically elected governments of reformers Jacobo Arbenz in Guatemala and Mohammed Mossadegh in Iran. Guatemalans got a repressive military junta, and Iranians saw the restoration of the U.S.-friendly Shah to the Peacock Throne.

It was a year for scientific miracles. Dr. Jonas Salk created a vaccine against polio. Drs. Francis Crick and James Watson described the structure of DNA as a double helix, and in Denmark, Dr. Christian Hamburger performed the world's first sex change operation on a young American G.I. named George Jorgensen.

This collection of letters from that eventful year casts a wide net over characters and events both fact and fiction. At the center of the action are a couple of characters who made their way from the Twenties and meet here for the first time: Nicholas Carraway, Republican functionary and one-time novelist, and Jacob Barnes, expatriate newsman. These gentlemen were previously thought to be the creations of a couple of novelists named F. Scott Fitzgerald and Ernest Hemingway, but it is revealed here for the first time that Nick and Jake are real historical figures. Fitzgerald and Hemingway never existed. That's our story, and we're sticking to it.

History has been tweaked and bent to suit our purposes, but a decent respect to the opinions of mankind has kept us close to the line of essential historical truths. Some of the most beloved works of 20th-century American literature have been cheerfully pillaged. Names have not been changed, and the innocent will have to shift for themselves.

NAMING NAMES

CHARACTER LEGEND
(in order of appearance)

Nick Carraway (The Great Gatsby): In his youth he wrote a novel; now he's a patriotic American who wants only to serve his country ... if his country still has a place for him.

Jake Barnes (The Sun Also Rises): Expatriate, legendary journalist, he's covered Europe for three decades. Once he thought of writing a novel, but never got beyond telling his story late at night to a sympathetic bartender.

George/Christine Jorgensen (sex-change pioneer): She's looked at life from both sides now, and she knows secrets of the heart ... and secrets that can spell trouble.

Allen Dulles (CIA director): As the first director of the fledgling CIA, he has ambitions to control the world ... if he can control his own associates.

Ronnie Gilchrist (Nick & Jake): You can take the girl out of Winnetka ... and with the right influences, you can take Winnetka out of the girl.

Irving Kristol (co-founder, Encounter; neo-conservative pioneer): Could the liberal editor of a leftist intellectual journal have a secret agenda?

Senator Joseph McCarthy (junior senator from Wisconsin): He had the Commies crying Uncle Sam ... until he took a shine to the army.

John Foster Dulles (Secretary of State): Ike's right hand, the Dulles who played by the book.

Margery Pyle Carraway (Nick & Jake): Nick's estranged wife--it was the little things that drove them apart.

Dorothy Kilgallen (newspaper columnist, radio/TV personality): Scandal was her line, the Little Red Thrush her mystery guest.

Alden Pyle Carraway (The Quiet American): Nick's son; expatriate, rebel, idealist; he did great harm out of good intentions.

Larry Darrell (The Razor's Edge): For him, the line between enlightenment and espionage was as thin as a razor's edge.

Irving Sheinbloom (A Mighty Wind): Folk music was his business, but a pretty girl could send him on top of Old Smokey.

Jackie Susann (author, Valley of the Dolls): From her room in the Martha Washington Hotel for Women, she had her own brand of New York savvy for Ronnie Gilchrist.

Little Johnny Phillips (founder, The Mamas and the Papas): Musically ahead of his time, come Monday morning he was still a kid.

Lee Hays and Ronnie Gilbert (The Weavers): Members of the popular folk quartet, they needed a replacement for Pete Seeger, but Ronnie Gilchrist was not to be their darling.

The other guy in the Weavers: Whose name no one could ever remember.

Roy M. Cohn (Senator McCarthy's top aide): He found Commie filth on every bookshelf, and a Red in every closet.

Davey Schine (McCarthy investigator): Did his heart belong to "Daddy," or did every little breeze seem to whisper Maurice?

Thomas Fowler (The Quiet American): British journalist. Saigon was his beat, Americans were his *bête*--especially the quiet ones.

Stephen Spender (British poet): A close Encounter with the CIA was more than he bargained for.

Robert Cohn (The Sun Also Rises): Roy's uncle, CIA maverick. He thought the sun also rose for him ... but only if he could make it set over Jake Barnes.

Maurice Chevalier (entertainer, collaborator): He sang for the Germans, but he didn't remember it well.

Clare Boothe Luce (author, ambassador): She could make Time stand still, but for Nick she was arsenic and old Luce.

Simone de Beauvoir and Jean-Paul Sartre (existentialists): These French intellectuals were more than willing to make Nick Carraway the toast of Paris.

Kim Philby (British/Soviet double agent): Could he be trusted with the deepest secrets of American intelligence?

Clyde Tolson (associate director, FBI): Special friend of the FBI Director, he knew all the secrets ... and he knew Christine.

Mary Richards (The Mary Tyler Moore Show): With Ronnie as her mentor, she would make it after all.

Bud Powell (American jazz pianist): A tormented genius who would do anything for a friend.

Francis Paudras (French jazz critic): Journalist, jazz lover, he would work till 'round midnight to help Jake.

Helen Fowler (The Quiet American): Thomas Fowler's estranged wife ... but no divorce.

Dr. Christian Hamburger (Danish surgeon): The Stein Ericksen of sex-change surgery.

Stein Ericksen (Olympic champion): The Christian Hamburger of Alpine skiing.

Jerry Wexler (record producer): Co-founder of Atlantic Records with **Ahmet Ertegun**, he had an ear for talent, and Ronnie Gilchrist was talent.

Ray Charles, Ruth Brown, LaVern Baker, Chuck Berry, David "Fathead" Newman (recording artists): They each had something to teach Ronnie about music ... and life.

Lady Brett Ashley (The Sun Also Rises): An old girlfriend of Jake's, she's chosen the path of enlightenment, but she hasn't lost her sense of entitlement.

Bill Buckley (author, conservative icon): A schoolyard bully.

Sloan Wilson (author, The Man in the Gray Flannel Suit): An American in Paris who picks up a novel idea from Nick.

James Baldwin (author): As an expatriate in another country, he was saving his fire for next time.

Lamont Cranston (The Shadow): A wealthy young man about town who uses his power to cloud men's minds to influence the course of history.

William Fromme (father of Manson Family member): Margery's husband-to-be, raising his daughter Lynette to be a squeaky-clean American patriot.

Dr. Mohammed Mossadegh (prime minister of Iran 1951-1953): He believed American-style democracy could change the Middle East.

Art Buchwald (journalist): A young protégé of Jake's at the Paris Tribune.

Shah Mohammed Reza Pahlevi (Shah of Iran): A young protégé of Allen Dulles's on the Peacock Throne.

Jimmie Dodd (host, The Mickey Mouse Club): A TV director with some Mickey Mouse ideas about what makes a show work.

Albert Camus (author, philosopher): Another French intellectual absurdly eager to champion Nick.

Howard Koch (screen writer): An American writer and exile of conscience from McCarthyism. Here's looking at you, kid.

Sen. Prescott Bush (senator, war profiteer): The Presidency--maybe not today, maybe not tomorrow, but soon and for the rest of your life.

George H. W. Bush (CIA desk officer): Can Dulles trust him?

Jean Renoir (movie director) and Yves Montand (movie star): They hope to make a movie version of Nick's gangster novel.

Francoise Sagan (author, Bonjour Tristesse): She flashes a certain smile at Nick, but he's not so certain.

Maurice Girodias (publisher, Venus in Bondage, The Story of O, Lolita, Lady Chatterley's Lover): He has no trouble in promising Nick an Olympian advance.

Gen. Raoul Salan (founder, Terrorist Group Against Algerian Independence): In case we need a Falangist takeover of France.

Edward R. Murrow (legendary pioneer of television journalism): He wants his old pal Jake to join him in a brave new enterprise in electronic journalism. Good night, and good luck.

Blossom Dearie (American jazz singer): American expatriate who takes Ronnie under her wing.

York Harding (The Quiet American): A writer of books, he helped Alden understand the role of the West.

THE LETTERS

Nicholas Carraway
Assistant Undersecretary of State for European Affairs
Department of State
Washington, D.C.

Mr. Jacob Barnes
Paris Herald Tribune
38, rue de Berri
Paris 16e, France

January 26, 1953

Dear Mr. Barnes,

We have not met, but I'm a great admirer of yours. I am an avid reader of your byline in the Trib, and one of the treasured books in my library is your memoir of Paris in the Twenties, A Lost Generation. It's clear to me that you have a greater understanding than most Americans of Europe, and of France in particular.

From your vantage point you will see the urgent need, in a world still recovering from the wounds of war, of spreading abroad the good news of American ideals, American values, and American progress. We showed the world our might in the armed conflict; now, with the architect of that victory leading from the White House, we must seize the opportunity to show the world our compassion, our moral compass, our democratic ideals, and the beacon of hope that shines from Lady Liberty's torch. I am hoping that you can assist me in gathering some information that may prove helpful to your country. There is, as you know, a bit of hysteria in Washington these days over the influence of International Communism in U.S. libraries abroad. You and I are men of the world. We know how damaging this sort of heavy-handed Puritan zeal can be to American prestige abroad when it gets out of hand.

I wonder if you can help me by compiling an informal list of books in embassy libraries that might be considered objectionable, so we can make a few timely removals and defuse the situation before it gets embarrassing. I realize this is an imposition, but I hope you will see the merit in this kind of preemptive strike.

Very Truly Yours,

Nicholas Carraway
Assistant Undersecretary of State for
European Affairs

Jacob Barnes
Paris Herald Tribune
38, rue de Berri
Paris 16, France

Nicholas Carraway
Ass't Undersec. of State for European
Affairs
Department of State
Washington, D.C.

January 29, 1953

Dear Mr. Carraway,
I would sooner swim the Marne.

Yours Truly,

Jake Barnes

Jake Barnes
1 rue de Fleurus
Paris 6, France

Mr. George Jorgensen
Royal Hospital
Copenhagen, Denmark

Jan. 29

George--

Good luck with the operation.

Me? It's a damned interesting suggestion, but no thanks! I am sitting here in the Closerie des Lilas watching some Bryn Mawr girls get drunk on white wine and what unscrupulous restaurateurs assure them is absinthe, imagining themselves in the fairy tales their fairy college professors told them. I too am doing my damnedest to get a drunk on, thanks to your proposal. It gives me the willies to think about it. Please. I already gave at the office.

Not that I haven't been tempted to make some changes in my life. When Brett went to Nepal last year, I kept thinking I was the one who should become a goddamn Buddhist monk and disappear from the world. I sometimes wish I'd written the novel about her I wanted to write, instead of pissing it away on A Lost Generation. You know, I told the whole story of her and me and Cohn and that damned bullfighter to a bartender one night around two in the morning. The sonofabitch pretended to be interested, but he was probably really hoping I'd shut the hell up so he could close up and go back to a clean, well-lighted room. It must have sounded like a bunch of nada to him, but it was fine and true and the next day it was gone and I had nothing to show for it but the hangover. And then I walked into the Crillon Bar that night and met you. And I thought, now there is one hell of a novel just begging to be written. Watch out for writers, Georgie my girl. We'll eat you alive and suck the marrow from your bones. That at least is our intention. Sometimes I even disgust myself, but writing is a goddamn disease.

Anyway, Brett was all right. And you're all right, George. You're a swell guy, and I guess this may be the last time I'll be able to say that.

And me? Fuck it, I guess I'll wait for the day they can sew the goddamn thing back on. What about yours? You won't be using it.

Yours always,

Jake

Nicholas Carraway
Assistant Undersecretary of State for
European Affairs
Department of State
Washington, D.C.

Mr. Allen Dulles
Director, Central Intelligence Agency

Jan. 30, 1953

Dear Mr. Dulles,

I wrote Barnes as per our discussion. Enclosed please find a copy of his response. He's a bit talkier than General McAuliffe at Bastogne, but not by much.

This may be the wrong way to get to someone like Barnes. If the idea is to use important journalists to shape opinion in France, Barnes is our man. But we're not going to get to him just by waving the flag. I don't know much about Europe, but I read Barnes' book, A Lost Generation, and I guess all of us followed the reporting he and Murrow did during the war. This is a tough, independent-minded guy.

I'm not sure I'm the best man for this job. Do you have any contacts who are closer to Barnes? I know he's on the board of

Encounter, which is a leftish intellectual magazine edited by a guy named Irving Kristol. Maybe Kristol could help us? Or I'll be glad to take another stab at him, but next time let me use my own approach.

Very Truly Yours,

Nicholas Carraway
Assistant Undersecretary of State

FROM THE DESK OF:

ALLEN DULLES

By special courier
Feb 2, 1953

Carraway--

We don't have any connection with Kristol or anyone else at Encounter. So you're our man. Europe is crucial to our goals. Barnes is the key to setting that up. He's the most authoritative voice in our European press corps. People listen to what he has to say, and I'm counting on you to make sure he says the right things. I've got the feeling Barnes may know things he shouldn't, but we don't know what or how much. Is his head on straight? Can he cause problems? Does he have beans to spill? And is he likely to spill them?

Sure, try Barnes your way. You're the ad man--sell him. And didn't you write a book once, too? Give him the old literary brotherhood.

Make it work, Nick. We need to start shaping opinion now.

Dulles

Nicholas Carraway
Assistant Undersecretary of State for European Affairs
Department of State
Washington, D.C.

February 2, 1953

Dear Mr. Barnes,

The Marne can be pretty damn chilly this time of year. Let's see if we can't find another way.

I think I made a bad start, and I apologize for that. I'd like to excuse my clumsy approach by pleading new-boy jitters. I've just come on board here at State, and am trying to find out how I fit in. The first months of a new administration are more chaotic than I'd imagined, and we're all feeling our way along. I don't even know where the men's room is yet.

As I mentioned in my first letter, I'm a great admirer of your writing. A Lost Generation felt like what Paris in the Twenties must have been. It's a hell of a book, the real thing. And your dispatches from Europe, during the War and since, are better than anyone alive is doing. It's all given me the illusion of knowing a bit about you, and of course you know nothing at all about me. So I'll give you an autobiographical sketch by way of an introduction, if you'll indulge me. I'm a bit of a writer myself.

When I was a young man I lived for a season on the Eastern seaboard, among people who were privileged and careless and very rich. I grew up in the Midwest, and the Northeast had an irresistible lure to a boy lying on his bed looking out over twilit cornfields and cattle pastures, and dreaming of the center of the universe.

I came East in the fall of '16 to do my university work at New Haven, and from there only a few miles of railroad track separated me from my dreams of a fortune in the New York City bond market.

As it happened, I took the long way around. The Great War intervened, and with a minimum of reflection and an excess of romantic impulsiveness, I joined the Norton-Harjes ambulance service under the French--my carte d'identité shows a slim, tousle-haired boy with a dimpled jaw, a pendulous lower lip, and eyes as yet unacquainted with tragedy. Then, when America got into the War, I signed up for a crash course in the Serbo-Croatian language, and found myself assigned to General Pershing's staff as a translator/interrogator. I was close enough to the action to hear and smell it, but I never really had the chance to test myself under fire--or in the chilly waters of the Marne, though Lord knows I got to see them, eddying mud and blood. That memory will last me a good deal longer than my Serbo-Croatian. Things learned fast are forgotten fast. We never captured any Serbo-Croatians for me to interrogate, and I hardly remember a word of it. "Dobar dan, ja se zovem Lt. Carraway." That's about it.

But New York was still there after the Armistice, and upon my return I could think of no tempting alternative to trolling in the marts of money. I took a small cottage that summer on Long Island, from which I commuted to a brokerage firm on Wall Street. I wanted to be rich and careless like the people in whose circles I managed to move with diminishing comfort during that summer and autumn in the Twenties; most especially my immediate neighbor and friend, a man named Gatsby. But Gatsby died--was murdered actually--and my romance with a lady golfer soured, and finally I had to face the fact that I was out of my element there.

And so I came back to the Midwest, where I have lived ever since. I tried my hand at a few different careers--my family's hardware business was the first one, but I was no more suited to it than I'd imagined I would be. I wrote a novel drawn from my experiences in the East, which brought me a brief flare of literary success. I parlayed that into a stint as a journalist at the Chicago Tribune, but soon discovered there were men--such as yourself--who were much better at it than I. After that, I took a short fling at the restaurant business, and even, God help me, spent eight months at the selling of used automobiles.

Then a man I had known at Yale struck up a conversation on the golf course one afternoon that led to our opening an advertising shop in Chicago. Advertising was a wide-open field in those days, and through a combination of ignorance and luck we managed to make a pretty good thing of it. Taylor & Carraway today has branches in Minneapolis and Milwaukee in addition to the home office on Fair Street, with billings of over six million.

We even handled a piece of the Eisenhower campaign, and I spent some time with Allen Dulles, whom I had known in France in '18. Dulles asked me if I'd be interested in a stint of government service when Ike took office (he was very confident about that!) Said his brother was in line for State in an Eisenhower administration. I told him I'd think about it, and next thing I knew I had a job in Washington, and a leave of absence from the firm.

So here I am, with an office in Foggy Bottom and not the foggiest idea what I'm doing here, other than trying to do a bit of good in terms of selling the American message abroad and helping the Europeans understand what we're all about. It will be a great help to me if I can mine the brains and experiences of men like you, who have lived abroad long enough to have a European's view of what it is America represents. But I would be dissembling if I didn't add that in your case, the motivation is more personal. As I've said before, I'm a great fan of your writing. I have a copy of A Lost Generation here in my Washington office. And as much as anything else, I'm frankly hoping to take advantage of the cachet of my moment in the halls of power to strike up a correspondence with one of my literary heroes.

This has been more long-winded than I ever intended. If you're still reading at this point, I hope we can start from scratch and keep in touch.

Very Truly Yours,

Nicholas Carraway

Mlle Christine Jorgensen
Royal Hospital
Copenhagen, Denmark

3 February

Dear Jake,

Language, language! Remember, I'm a lady now.

Thanks for your note. Yes, I'm fine. Sore as hell, but fine. More than fine. Wonderful. Terrified, but wonderful. So much to get used to! I keep bursting into tears, and I'm not even unhappy. I'm ecstatically happy. I wish I knew what the hell was going on.

It has been the most extraordinary journey, and I am just now arriving on the shores of an amazing, exotic land. I always assumed, vaguely and romantically, that once I crossed that border, I would be truly at home, and I'd feel at home right away.

And in a way, that's true. My body fits me now, as it never did before. All the parts feel right. But what else fits? I used to love playing dress-up when I was little--drove my Dad crazy. And for the past year or so, as I started trying to prepare myself for this leap into the unknown, I dressed more and more the way I wanted to be. But in a way, it was still playing dress-up.

Now it's real, and it's scarier than I thought it would be. Now I have to get it right. Everyone will be looking at me, looking for any mistake.

But you, Jake. You have demons of your own, don't you? Despite being the gruff old bear who walks by himself and doesn't need anything from anybody. Sew it back on? What an idea! You're more than welcome to mine. It may smell a little of formaldehyde, but ... I wonder!

I'll put you in touch with Dr. Hamburger.

Warmest Regards,

Christine

Ronnie Gilchrist
Snicklepoo and the Baby Sitter
WGKG Chicago

February 4, 1953

Dear Mr. Carraway,

The strangest thing. I got a letter from Senator McCarthy's committee asking me to come and testify. I can't imagine what they think I can help them with, though of course, I'll help in any way I can. Do you know Senator McCarthy?

Congratulations again on your new job. Mr. Taylor has been wonderful in giving me advice about the show, but I know it never would have worked as well as it did without you. I still have these urges to tinker with the show, like singing some new songs. There are some awfully cute ones out now, like that one about the doggie in the window. And I was just looking at some darling polka dot fabric that would make a cute new bowtie for Snicklepoo, but I keep reminding myself of what you said about not changing a thing. Well, you know me. The eternal worry wart. If I were in Washington, I'd probably be tinkering with the Constitution and the Declaration of Independence.

I'll be in Washington at the end of the week. I'll be staying at the YWCA. It would be wonderful to see you while I'm there--and Mrs. C., of course--but I know how busy you must be running the country.

Your friend,

Ronnie Gilchrist

Jacob Barnes
Paris Herald Tribune
38, rue de Berri
Paris 16, France

February 6

Carraway:

Oh, you're that Nicholas Carraway? Yes, I read your novel about the gangster. It wasn't as bad a novel as the critics later made it out to be, but it was a very poor novel.

Barnes

Jake Barnes
1 rue de Fleurus
Paris 6, France

Feb. 6

Dear George, or I guess it's Mlle. Christine now?

Don't do anything too fast. I've been getting the damnedest letters from a State Department flack named Nicholas Carraway. Started by asking me about subversive books in overseas libraries--what the hell is that all about? These guys think they own the press. Any pipe dreams we had about Ike coming in and sweeping the Tail-gunner aside are looking like hashish now. Especially with the Dulles Brothers running things.

But Carraway interests me, and I'll tell you why.

The guy is a writer, or used to be. Wrote a swell novel about a thousand years ago, by the name of Trimalchio in West Egg. It was damn good, well written, and true. He gave his character an inner honesty that said more about the best and worst in America than I ever expected to see from our godforsaken generation. What's damn ironic, considering his first letter to me, is that

I ordered a bunch of copies of it when I was in charge of purchasing for the Voice of America.

Anyway, now he's telling me the story of his life. The Reader's Digest condensed version: He sold out.

There's something sad about him, as there is with most sellouts. I wonder if he still has a chance to make it right. There aren't too goddamned many second acts to American lives. Be nice to think his could be one of them.

If not, maybe the second act is another Carraway I just met recently, this one with the first name Alden. Jimmy Baldwin introduced me, so he's probably a queer --fit right in with your velvet mafia in Washington. Just as likely a Red, too. Certainly an idealist. But I liked him. He submitted an article to me for Encounter. Fuzzy thinking, but he can write. I'm sending it on to Kristol, with a recommendation that we publish it. Wonder if the kid's any relation to the State Department Carraway? Wouldn't surprise me. But then nothing surprises me anymore. Fuck it, George--sorry, Chris--Carraway's book was good. He was a damn sight too bowled over by the rich, which is probably why he sold out. Still is, apparently. Made a point of telling me his agency billed six fucking million a year.

Well, I'm not telling him I liked his book. It'd just encourage him. He wants to be friends, and old Barnyard Jake has all the friends he needs. I'll keep on being rude to the poor slob. Maybe he'll go the hell away. Listen lady, write to me. I want to know how you're doing with the new plumbing. When are you going to be up and around?

Yr Man of Mystery,

Jake

MEMORANDUM

2/6/53
Memo from: Jake Barnes
To: Irving Kristol

Sending along a manuscript by a kid who's been bombarding me with them. Name's Alden Carraway. Raw, simple prose, and a nodding acquaintance with truth. Reminds me of me when I was younger, only I got over it. He's got this idea that the personal is the political and vice versa. Naive, but provocative. Hope you like it, you goddamned cynic.

He's in a lather over the situation in Iran. He's been hanging out with some expat Persians in the Latin Quarter, and he's fallen in love with Mossadegh and his People's Government over there in Iran. (Which he seems to think the U.S. is planning to pull the rug out from under.) Not sure how solid his information is, but I'm also not sure he's wrong. I've got some sources I'm going to shake a little and see what falls out of the tree.

The kid can write, though. He's come up with a catchy name for the underdeveloped countries--he calls them "The Third World." He uses the term to refer to the unaligned nations, the ones who're neither in our net nor the Russkis', and it's got a sly reference to the Third Estate, the Great Unwashed of the French Revolution. Not bad, eh?

Odd coincidence--I've gotten a couple of letters from another Carraway, a stuffed shirt in the Eisenhower administration. Wrote a pretty good novel about a hundred years ago, name of Trimalchio in West Egg. Turns out he's the kid's father. Offspring doesn't think much of the old fart. Hypocrite, sellout--you know. Wonder what kids of ours would have to do to rebel? Become right wing crypto-fascists and bundists, I guess. That reminds me--I hear you and Bea are expecting. Congratulations, I guess.

Barnes

ENCOUNTER
New York, NY

February 10, 1953

Jake,

Thanks for the congratulations, I guess. I'll read the young lion's manuscript. Look, don't bother with the Iran thing. I've heard those rumors too, they're bullshit. You can hear a dozen others sitting around the coffee houses and beer halls where the kids hang out.

Meanwhile, here's something you may find interesting. This, of course, like so much correspondence and cocktail party conversation these days, relates to the junior senator from Wisconsin. He fills the lineaments of a thug, sometimes to comic effect, and this transcript from a recent hearing may amuse you--especially since it relates to your pen pal Carraway. It comes from the testimony of a young lady named Ronnie Gilchrist, who appears to have the demeanor (and intellectual capacity) of a kindergarten teacher. (The underlines and marginal notes, of course, are mine--the committee stenographer has no sense of irony.)

McCarthy: Please state your name for the record.

Gilchrist: Veronica Edith Gilchrist.

McCarthy: But that's not the name you use, is it?

Gilchrist: People call me Ronnie.

McCarthy: People call you ... ?

Gilchrist: Everybody does. My parents, my friends ... it's a nickname.

McCarthy: Come on, Miss Gilbert. Isn't it a fact ... isn't it a fact that you hide behind this alias, as if you have been deliberately trying to hide your true identity?

(You've got to read it with that flat Midwestern twang of his--isn't it a fact ... isn't it a fact ... priceless!)

Gilchrist: No, I just ... Ronnie just seems friendlier ...

McCarthy: Friendlier? Are you telling this committee that you desire to be friendly?

Gilchrist: Well, yes, of course.

McCarthy: Friendly as in a friendly witness for the committee, or friendly as in ... Comrade?

Gilchrist: Huh?

Cohn: Mr. Chairman, the witness is being unresponsive.

McCarthy: Witness is directed to answer the question.

McCarthy: Never mind. I think we can all figure out the answer. Miss Gilbert ... Miss so-called Ronnie Gilbert--I hand you this piece of paper and ask you to read the words on it.

Gilchrist: (reading) I was at Franklin Roosevelt's side / Just a while before he died / He said, "One world must come out of World War II, / Yankee, Russian, white or tan, / Lord, a man is just a man, / We're all brothers and we're only passing through." ... Oh, now I understand ...

McCarthy: You understand? You understand this dirty, Communistic, unpatriotic piece of Red garbage? Well, that's very interesting, Ronnie, because most Americans ... most real Americans ...

would not understand such a piece of verminous treason.

(My God, verminous--don't you love it?)

Gilchrist: No ... I meant ... I understand how you got confused. This is a song by the Weavers--"Passing Through." The girl in the Weavers is Ronnie Gilbert. I'm Ronnie Gilchrist.

McCarthy: Are you trying to tell the committee that you don't know the words to this song?

Gilchrist: Oh, yes. We used to sing it at camp. We never sang that verse, though.

McCarthy: What are some of the verses you did sing at this indoctrination camp?

Gilchrist: (starting to cry) It was Girl Scout camp!

Cohn: Mr. Chairman, the witness is being unresponsive.

McCarthy: Witness is directed to answer the question.

Gilchrist: What ...

McCarthy: I'll repeat the question, since you appear to have one of those convenient memory lapses that happen so often to Communists and fellow travelers. You tell the committee you do know the words to this Commie filth? Recite them for us. You ... heh-heh ... you don't have to sing ...

(Appreciative ripple of laughter from the gallery. The guy can work a crowd!)

Gilchrist: Well, it starts "I was with George Washington ... "

McCarthy: I want it noted in the record that these Commies will stop at nothing to infiltrate our great American patriotic heritage. Miss Gilbert ...

Gilchrist: (in a squeaky whisper) Gilchrist.

McCarthy: Miss Gilbert, what are the names of your pals in this so-called singing group, the Weavers?

Gilchrist: Their names?

(Committee Counsel Roy Cohn whispers to Sen. McCarthy. I don't know about that Cohn--smart as hell, but a weasel.)

McCarthy: Is there some reason why you don't want to tell us their names?

Gilchrist: No, of course not. I want to help the committee. But I'm not ...

McCarthy: You say you want to help the Committee. But you refuse to give us their names?

Gilchrist: No ... I ... let's see ... there's Pete Seeger ...

(Cohn whispers.)

McCarthy: The well-known Communist.

Gilchrist: And Lee Hays ...

(And Cohn again.)

McCarthy: The well-known Communist.

Gilchrist: And Ronnie Gilbert ... and I can't remember the other.

McCarthy: Come on now, Ronnie.

Gilchrist: (sobbing) I ...

McCarthy: Come on. You're doing fine. This Committee wants to believe you. This Committee is here to help you and all patriotic Americans. We know there are a lot of fellow travelers like you who've seen the light, and are now ready to defend America. What about you, Ronnie? Do you want to help defend America?

Gilchrist: Yes ... oh, yes!

McCarthy: Yes, what?

Gilchrist: I want to help defend America.

McCarthy: Okay, then. You've given us this Seeger. Good. You've given us this Hays. Good. Why do you continue to refuse to give us the other name?

Gilchrist: (still sobbing) I can't ... I can't remember!

(Cohn again.)

(And again.)

McCarthy: Well, don't worry, sister. We'll get to the bottom of this. I have no more questions of this witness, Mr. Chairman. I think it's pretty clear where she stands.

Gilchrist: No! No! I'm a good American! I hate the Communists! I ... I ... I know somebody in President Eisenhower's administration!

McCarthy: And who would this be, Miss Gilbert?

Gilchrist: Mr. Nicholas Carraway--he's in the State Department!

(Silence in the room. A long whispered conference between Cohn and McCarthy. Notes are written down.)

McCarthy: Request a subpoena be issued in the name of Mr. Nicholas Carraway.

(ENCRYPTED AND DECODED)
(2/10)

FROM: IRVING KRISTOL
TO: ALLEN DULLES

BARNES MAKING NOISES ABOUT NOSING INTO IRAN. I'VE LAUGHED HIM OFF IT, BUT HE COULD MAKE TROUBLE.

--KRISTOL

(ENCRYPTED AND DECODED)
(2/11)

FROM: ALLEN DULLES
TO: IRVING KRISTOL
TOP SECRET

BE CAREFUL WITH BARNES. HE SMELLS SOMETHING, AND I'M NOT READY TO TAKE A CHANCE ON BRINGING HIM INTO THIS YET. HE'S SMART, SO WATCH YOUR STEP. ENCOUNTER IS A KEY PART OF OPERATION ELBA. WE HAVE THE NATIONAL STUDENT ASSOCIATION COVERED, AND BETWEEN THAT AND ENCOUNTER WE CAN STIR UP TROUBLE, AND KEEP MONITORING IT AT THE SAME TIME.

IF WE KEEP ENOUGH LEFTIST AGITATION GOING IN FRANCE, THAT'LL KEEP THE RIGHT CHASING THEIR TAILS, WHICH MEANS NO CHANCE OF A

STABLE GOVERNMENT. WHICH MEANS NO ONE TO KEEP A HANDLE ON THE WAR IN INDO-CHINA. THE COMMUNIST THREAT WILL START TO MAKE AMERICANS NERVOUS, BUT IT WON'T REALLY HAPPEN UNTIL AFTER IKE'S WOUND UP TWO TERMS, AND A DEMOCRAT GETS IN.

THE DEMOCRATS INHERIT A QUAGMIRE, AND BY 1964, YOUR NEOCONSERVATIVE COUNTERREVOLUTION SHOULD HAVE ALL ITS DUCKS LINED UP, AND WE CAN SWEEP INTO POWER BEHIND NIXON. IF NIXON SELF-DESTRUCTS, WE MIGHT LOOK AT THAT GUY FROM ARIZONA, GOLDWATER.

IT'S A FOOLPROOF PLAN. AND IF THE DEMOCRATIC PRESIDENT TURNS OUT TO BE TOO POPULAR (BUT I FIGURE IT'LL BE HARRIMAN, SO THAT'S NOT TOO LIKELY) ... WELL, THERE ARE WAYS OF DEALING WITH THAT, TOO.

SO, FOR NOW, STAY IN PLACE. AS FOR THE POSITION YOU SHOULD BE TAKING ON IRAN, PRO-MOSSADEGH, ALL THE WAY. WE DON'T WANT TO TIP OUR HAND THAT WE'RE EVEN CONSIDERING ANOTHER OPTION. SO DON'T WORRY ABOUT PUBLISHING WOOLLY HEADED YOUNG LEFTIES--THAT WORKS PERFECTLY. REMEMBER, WE'RE BUILDING A WORLD IN WHICH OUR KIDS WILL CALL THE SHOTS.

DULLES

Jacob Barnes
Paris Herald Tribune
38, rue de Berri
Paris 16, France

Feb. 13

Carraway--

I knew a Jimmy Gatz, back in Kansas City when I was a cub reporter. He was collecting for a loan shark. I used him as a source a few times. He talked more than he should have, and I thought he was too much of a dreamer to make it in the rackets. I wondered what had happened to him. You got some things wrong about him, but I recognized the Jimmy I knew in your Gatsby character.

So what do you want to know about the International Red Menace?

Barnes

FROM THE DESK OF:

ALLEN DULLES

By special courier
Feb. 15, 1953

Carraway--

So--Barnes is nibbling. Good work. Good work. For the time being, just play out the line. Concentrate on strengthening your ties with the man. Get into his confidence. We can reel him in later.

Dulles

Nicholas Carraway
Assistant Undersecretary of State for European Affairs
Department of State
Washington, DC.

February 17, 1953

Dear Mr. Barnes,

So you knew Gatz? I don't wonder you feel I got some things wrong about him. I no longer remember what was Gatz and what was Gatsby and what was just my youthful romantic imagination.

Don't worry about the libraries. As I said, I'm just learning this job, and I've been sending out a lot of letters inherited from my predecessors. But Lord knows the Red Menace is real enough, as you should know, being cheek to jowl over there with the countries that have been closed off by the Iron Curtain.

I've been called to testify this week at the McCarthy hearings. A friendly witness, they assure me. As I have every intention of being. My cordial invitation bears the personal signature of Roy Cohn, the Chairman's right hand. While I wouldn't deny that the senator has a touch of the bull in the china shop to him at times, I'm sure his intentions are patriotic. Liberals like to paint him as a fanatical clown, but there are Communists, Barnes, and they are a threat to the security of this country. One of these days I hope I can try to convince you of that over a martini on the Champs Elysees.

Meanwhile, I'll wander over to the Hill on Thursday and see what the committee wants to talk to me about, and be what help I can.

Yours Truly,

Nick Carraway

New York Herald Tribune
PARIS EDITION, FEBRUARY 17, 1953

THE BARNES DOOR

PARIS--When Dr. Mohammed Mossadegh was elected Premier of Iran, the first thing he did was nationalize his country's oil industry. There may be easier ways of sorting out your friends from your enemies, but this one did the job.

The Iranians thought it was a fine idea. The oil, after all, was Iranian. But the British cried foul. The oil companies, after all, were British. The oil fields might belong to Iran, but the drills and the pumps had John Bull's name tags on them. His Majesty's government sued. The Brits took the matter to the United Nations. Dr. Mossadegh went to New York and won his case before the Security Council. Then he went to The Hague to defend the takeover, and he won again in the World Court.

Dr. Mossadegh stopped in Paris on his way home from the Netherlands, and he sat down for a few minutes with this newspaper. He is a quiet, frail man, who projects the aggrieved air of a beagle hound shut up in a hot car. But when he talks about his country, his eyes light up, and he leans forward like a preacher in his pulpit.

"Democracy is possible in the Middle East," he said. "It is as your Mr. Jefferson put it so eloquently, there comes a time in the course of human events when it becomes necessary for one people to dissolve the political bands which have connected them with another ... "

Nobody likes to lose something they think of as their own. From time to time whispers reach us of plans for a British invasion of Iran, which seems unlikely. We've also heard rumors of a coup sponsored by Britain. That sounds more plausible. But Dr. Mossadegh enjoys the backing of something like 98 percent of the people of his country, so a popular uprising against him may be a hard story to sell.

Where did Dr. Mossadegh get a crazy idea like nationalizing the oil industry? He says he got it from the British.

"They are nationalizing their steel industry," he pointed out, "and their railroads. They tell us it is different for them, that they are an advanced civilization. My ancestors were civilized when Winston Churchill's ancestors wore skins and lived in caves. My only crime is that I removed from this land the network of colonialism and the political and economic influence of the greatest empire on earth."

Some of the whispers that have reached us have the British looking to America for help with their problem. What business is it of ours? It isn't. If anybody tells you it is, tell him to look up what America stands for. We stand up for the little guy. We stand up for the poor, the downtrodden, the huddled masses yearning to breathe free. Undercutting democracy is not America's style. Never has been, and please God, never will be. We leave empire to the empire-builders, and colonialism to the colonialists.

ENCOUNTER
New York, NY

Irving Kristol
February 20

Well, Barnes, I just read through the latest transcripts from the McCarthy hearings, and your friend Carraway seems to have run into a Mack truck at the committee. Enclosed is the truck. You'll enjoy this exchange with the junior senator from Wisconsin.

McCarthy: Mr. Carraway, I, uh ... Mr. Carraway, will you tell this committee how you were employed before you came to the State Department?

Carraway: Certainly, Senator. I am a partner in the advertising firm of Taylor and Carraway, based in Chicago. We've got an office up in your neck of the woods, too--Milwaukee. I'm on leave from that outfit right now, and I hope they won't change the locks on me while I spend a little time working for the government.

McCarthy: (laughs) I'm sure they won't. Mr. Carraway ... do you employ any known Communists at your advertising firm?

Carraway: No sir, I do not.

McCarthy: None at all, Mr. Carraway? Are you quite sure of that?

Carraway: Of course I am. Do you have evidence that I am mistaken?

McCarthy: We'll have no more of that, Mr. Carraway. You will answer the question.

Carraway: Senator, I'm here at the committee's invitation, and I mean to help in any way I can.

McCarthy: I, uh ... I think it might be better for you, Carraway, if you just came out with it yourself. That is, if you don't have anything to hide ...

Carraway: With all due respect, Senator, I am being as responsive as I possibly can.

McCarthy: In other words, Carraway, you refuse to tell this committee about the Reds you do business with in this little advertising game of yours?

Carraway: Damn it, Senator, stop your insinuations! If you have something to say, say it!

Cohn: (whispering) He's covering up, like they all do. Hit him with the testimony.

(Roy Cohn hands a document to Sen. McCarthy.)

McCarthy: I show you the testimony of a young woman in the entertainment business, a well-known Communist named Ronnie Gilbert, who names you as a close associate ...

Carraway: Ronnie Gil ... oh, you mean Ronnie Gilchrist. Sure, she's a good kid. She does a children's show for us. A Communist? Senator, I don't know who does your investigating, but if it's Mr. Cohn, I suggest you take away his Junior G-Man kit.

(Cohn turns a lovely shade of red, something on the order of a '47 Margaux.)

Cohn: Look here, Carraway ...

McCarthy: Mr. Carraway, Mr. Cohn is our chief counsel, and he is entitled to normal courtesy.

Caraway: My apologies, Mr. Cohn.

McCarthy: What about this little Red thrush, Nick? Did you ever ask her if she was a Communist?

Carraway: No.

McCarthy: Weren't you curious? If somebody told me an associate of mine was a Communist, I'd get on the phone and say, 'What about this? Is this true?'

Carraway: Nobody ever told me she was a Communist! Senator, that little girl hasn't got a political bone in her body. She's about as subversive as Snow White!

McCarthy: Nick, we're going to give you a chance to redeem yourself here. Can you tell us, of your own knowledge, about anyone else, in or out of government, who may have had trysts with this little Red thrush, from whom she may have extracted information that could be useful to the enemies of our country?

Carraway: No! Damn it, McCarthy ...

McCarthy: Let me shift to another line of questioning, Nickie. Would you like to tell this committee about your associations with known gangsters?

Carraway: I ... what?

McCarthy: Oh, come on, Carraway. Meyer Wolfsheim? Does that name ring any bells? James Gatz?

Well, those are the highlights. The Daily Mirror ran a story under the headline, TOP IKE MAN IN LOVE NEST WITH "LITTLE RED THRUSH." I don't know about the thrush, but where there's smoke, there's fire. You can forget Carraway. He won't be playing you the National Anthem any more. He's as washed up as last week's laundry.

Kristol

From the desk of:

JOHN FOSTER DULLES

February 20, 1953

Mr. Carraway,

As you know, we expect those in whom President Eisenhower places his trust to be completely forthcoming about their associations. Senator McCarthy has raised serious questions about yours. The State Department wishes to be fair, but we will need to see a much fuller explanation from you.

Yours truly,

John Foster Dulles
Secretary of State

Mrs. Nicholas Carraway
40125 Oak Park Drive
Oak Park, Illinois

February 21, 1953

Nicholas,

I've always had my suspicions about you and your little Red thrush. I'm only amazed that you thought you could pull the wool over the eyes of a man like Senator McCarthy.

A woman has a right to expect a man who'll take care of her and put her on a pedestal, just the way our country has a right to expect people to honor her values and our American way of life. Well, I'm keeping the house, and the car, and all our possessions. I deserve them.

A locksmith is here today, changing the locks on all of the doors, and installing an alarm system. It used to be safe to leave your door unlocked in this town. No more. Children used to respect their elders. You used to be able to walk down the street, and every kid you saw, you knew who their family was, and they'd tip their caps or give a little curtsey, just as if the whole village was part of bringing them up. But that's another thing the damn Communists have taken away from us.

I knew when I married you that you had "artistic" tendencies--that silly book--but I let myself believe you had put it all behind you. I suppose love is blind. I should have seen it all along. The way our son has turned into a wild-eyed Bohemian just breaks my heart. Certainly Alden didn't take after my side of the family. The Pyles are decent stock.

I don't understand how General Eisenhower could have appointed a man like you to a position of influence. Senator Taft never would have done it. I never trusted Eisenhower. You do know how cozy he was with the Russians during the war. Well, I believe the country is coming to its senses, and Senator McCarthy will be our next president. From now on, you may direct all contact with me to my lawyers, Quayle and Quayle.

With no affection,

Margery Carraway

A NEW YORK JOURNAL AMERICAN EXCLUSIVE

by DOROTHY KILGALLEN

February 22, 1953

STATE DEPT. PINKO, LITTLE RED THRUSH IN CONSPIRACY

This reporter has learned of a secret correspondence between "Little Red Thrush" Ronnie Gilbert and Nicholas Carraway, the State Department Commie recently unmasked by the McCarthy Committee. We have obtained a copy of a letter in which the Thrush tells Pinko Nicko, "If I were in Washington, I'd probably be tinkering with the Constitution and the Declaration of Independence."

From the desk of:

JOHN FOSTER DULLES

February 23, 1953

Mr. Carraway:

I expect your letter of resignation on my desk by 5:00 PM today.

John F. Dulles

Secretary of State

Nicholas Carraway
c/o YMCA
1711 Rhode Island Avenue NW
Washington, DC

Feb. 26

Dear Margery,

After all the catastrophic events of the last ten days, your bombshell is neither the most unexpected nor, if truth be told, the most wounding. If we are both honest, we'll admit that this breakup has been a long time coming. Our marriage has been an abandoned battlefield for many years now.

I don't think we need to quarrel over the division of spoils. I shan't want much. I have enough clothes here in Washington. I've instructed Dick Daley to sort out the money and property and to make sure you have everything you need and want.

As for my "Little Red Thrush," as you and the press and that idiot McCarthy delight in calling Miss Gilchrist, she is as innocent in all this as a songbird struck by a speeding train. The idea of my having had an affair with that young lady would be laughable if the effect of all this weren't so tragic. She has, I would guess, less knowledge of sex than you do. That our conjugal life managed to produce a son proves, I think, the existence if not of Divine Miracles then at least of a Cosmic Sense of Humor.

My immediate plans are vague. I only know that they call for putting an ocean between me and the country that until a week ago I served without reservation. I still believe in this country, but at the moment the evidence suggests that it does not think much of me.

If you should have any reason to get in touch with me, you can write care of the Guarantee Trust Co. in Paris. I'm going to try to find Alden and see what I can do about making up for things.

A good marriage is a terrible thing to waste. Ours, however, is one the world will little note, nor long remember.

Yours, Nick

(ENCRYPTED AND DECODED)
(2/24)
FROM: IRVING KRISTOL
TO: ALLEN DULLES

DO WE NEED SOMEONE ELSE TO SHADOW BARNES? IT LOOKS AS THOUGH CARRAWAY'S OUT OF THE PICTURE. OR ARE YOU WORKING WITH MCCARTHY ON THIS?

KRISTOL

(ENCRYPTED AND DECODED)
(2/25)
FROM: ALLEN DULLES
TO: IRVING KRISTOL

WORK WITH MCCARTHY? IT WOULD BE EASIER TO WORK WITH GARGANTUA. BUT MCCARTHY CAN BE A USEFUL IDIOT. HE'S DROPPED A GIFT INTO OUR LAP RE: OPERATION ELBA WITH THIS CARRAWAY BUSINESS. IT'S A PERFECT COVER FOR C. TO INGRATIATE HIMSELF WITH THE LEFTIES. RIGHT NOW HE'S FEELING LIKE A SAFE FELL ON HIM. WE'LL LET HIM LICK HIS WOUNDS ON HIS OWN, TO KEEP HIM CONVINCING, BEFORE WE BRING HIM IN AND BRIEF HIM. BUT HE'S A COMPANY MAN. HE'LL PLAY BALL.

DULLES

Ile de France
February 28
Somewhere at sea

Mr. Alden Carraway
C/o American Embassy
Paris

Dear Alden,

I'm sure you'll have heard by now about your father and the McCarthy hearings. I still don't understand it. You'd think a man who had served his country and his family with such conspicuous colorlessness would be spared the indignity of these wild accusations of love nests, Communist conspiracy, and high treason.

I'm on board the Ile de France, sailing for Paris. Right now I have an overwhelming need to get away, not just from Washington, but from everything familiar. It's not so much that I am feeling the disgrace. For some curious reason that doesn't seem to bother me as much as it should. Men I've known for years are suddenly crossing the street to avoid me, and somehow I find the uncrowded side of the street much more agreeable than I would have thought. I have more the sensation of going toward something than running away.

We'll have a good talk when I see you, which I hope will be soon. I will be staying at the George V, and I hope to be able to buy you dinner and begin a long and very important process of making things right between us.

Your Loving Father

PS. Your mother and I have separated.

FROM: NICHOLAS CARRAWAY
ABOARD THE ILE DE FRANCE D T
TO: JACOB BARNES, PARIS HERALD TRIBUNE
3/3/53

ARRIVING PARIS THURSDAY UNDER CLOUD STOP
IF STILL SPEAKING TO PARIAH CONTACT HOTEL
GEORGE V
CARRAWAY

Alden Carraway
219 rue de Vaugirard
Paris 15th

3 March

Dear Mr. Barnes,

It has been a while since you've heard from me and had to deal with my submissions to Encounter. You were kind enough to take me seriously and give me some encouragement, and for that I'm very grateful.

I just wanted to let you know that I'm leaving Paris, and it will probably be a while before I try writing anything for publication again. I met an amazing guy at the Dome a couple of weeks ago, an American named Larry Darrell. I don't know how to describe him to you--he was kind of bohemian in his dress, with a threadbare coat patched at the elbows, no hat or tie. His hair needed cutting, and he wore a full beard that showed signs of gray. But his smile was dazzling--white, even teeth, and dark eyes that seemed to start somewhere way back deep in his head. There was a look in those eyes that I can't explain, except to say that you felt like they knew something, or very likely everything.

We got to talking. I told him I was a writer. He listened to me spout my ideas about politics and social inequality, and he didn't say much, but I had the feeling that my words were being drawn into some profound and infinite space, as if he were not just hearing me but absorbing me into something universal. I know this will sound ridiculous to you, Mr. Barnes, but I was impressed and a bit unsettled. I realized that I was talking to someone who had actually been to the places I was only writing about. What did I know about the "Third World"? What was I doing, trying to tell anyone else about it?

We met again a few days later, and he told me a bit about himself, about how as a young man he had traveled to India and spent some time in an "ashram" there. He'd achieved something he called enlightenment, which I don't begin to understand, but I can tell you that the effect it seems to have produced in him is something we all could use a bit of.

Anyway, I've decided to give up writing and Paris and political causes for the time being, and head East to see if I can find some of this enlightenment stuff for myself. I don't know where exactly this search will take me, but I'll try to keep in touch and let you know how I'm doing. Again, I appreciate all your help and belief in me.

Yours Truly,

Alden Carraway

PS. Apparently my father is coming to Paris. That's another reason I'm taking off.

Hotel George V

MESSAGE

EN VOTRE ABSENCE

March 5

Pour M. Carraway

De la part de M. Barnes

Carraway —

Jesus, what the hell are you thinking? You can't afford this place. I hope to Christ you haven't checked in already. The George fucking Sank? This is the Fifties, Carraway, not the Twenties, and they charge real money these days. I read the papers, I know your assets are tied up tighter than a priest's vasectomy. Make your excuses and get a cab. There's a swell little joint on the Rue St. Sulpice, across the river, not too bad if you don't need to extend your arms. Tell the driver Hotel de l'Odeon. They know me there. I booked you a room on the second floor — that's the first floor over here — it'll save hauling your luggage up more than one flight of stairs. Bienvenue a Paris. I'll call you tomorrow.

— Barnes

Jake Barnes
1 rue de Fleurus
Paris 6, France

Dear Chris,

Carraway going, Carraway coming. Young Alden writes to tell me he's chucking politics for enlightenment. He met up with Larry Darrell --you know, the chap who started Brett off on Eastern thought--and there went another young firebrand out to change the world. Perhaps it's all for the best. Who the hell knows.

I've met Darrell. He's good. He's very good. And sometimes the damn world does seem vanity of vanities, like the prophet says. The wind goeth toward the south, and turneth again to the north. The King Barnes version of the Good Book--product of a misspent youth. It's all horseshit, anyway--I don't know whether I give a damn what people believe in--but it matters to me that people have the guts to stand guard in a lonely outpost of the maquis, or to keep secrets for strangers they'll never see again. Who's to say Alden's wrong? But I keep punching anyway, against the bastards. Whoever they are.

Meanwhile, the father has arrived in Paris. Nick Carraway, who I told you about. Poor guy has had his belief system shot out from under him. The American Dream, Eisenhower edition, marginal notes by Tailgunner Joe McCarthy. I know how he feels, having been shot up a bit myself.

We're a fuckingly complicated generation, Chris--ripped untimely from the womb of innocence and thrust into a meat grinder. Hard to imagine if you weren't there. You've made a hell of an Odyssey, but going to Denmark was the smallest part of it. For us--me, Carraway, Darrell--leaving America was probably the biggest part. Those of us who never went back, it turns out we could never really leave it. Guys like Carraway who tried to go back, never really got there. It's all tied up with Einstein and relativity--you can't step in the same river twice. How's that for irony and pity?

Je t'embrasse,

Jake

Ronnie Gilchrist
1337 Primrose Lane
Winnetka, Illinois

Mr. Nicholas Carraway
C/O Guarantee Trust Co., Paris, France
March 10, 1953

Dear Mr. Carraway,

First of all, I'm so sorry for everything that's happened to you. I guess I just don't understand what can be going on in America if a man like you is accused of being un-American. My mother says where there's smoke there's fire, and I keep trying to tell her that Senator McCarthy said some terrible things about me, too, but she just pretends she's not listening. When I tell her that I lost my TV show because of it, she says that was all your fault. But I know that's not true. I know you're the finest man I ever met, and if America has turned its back on you, well, there must be something wrong with America, that's all I can say.

So much has happened since I last wrote you, and some of it's been exciting, but it's all left me very confused. I'm not sure what to do, and I wondered if I could turn to you for advice. After I left Washington, and came back to Winnetka, I got a call from Mr. Irving Sheinbloom in New York!!!!! If you don't know who he is, he's a major figure in the Folk Music field! He wants me to come to New York and talk to him, he says he has some wonderful ideas for a new career for me. I told him that I was afraid no one wanted to hear so much as my name any more, but he said that in New York that would all be different.

I hope you don't mind me writing to you, after all that's happened. If you do, just tell me Ronnie, go away, and I'll understand. I do feel so terrible knowing it was me who dragged your name into this.
I hope you're liking France. I would love to go to France or Europe one day.

Your Friend,

Ronnie Gilchrist

4/12/53

FROM: I. KRISTOL
ENCOUNTER MAGAZINE, NY

TO: LAWRENCE DARRELL
POSTE RESTANTE
LHASA, TIBET

DARRELL
HOW ARTICLE ON INDOCHINA COMING?

KRISTOL

4/12/53

FROM: LAWRENCE DARRELL
POSTE RESTANTE
LHASA, TIBET

TO: ALLEN DULLES
CENTRAL INTELLIGENCE AGENCY
WASHINGTON, DC

DULLES--
MAY HAVE SOMEONE FOR YOU

DARRELL

Nicholas Carraway
Hotel de l'Odeon
14 March 1953

Dear Miss Gilchrist,

Please don't think of trying to shoulder the blame for this sorry turn of events. I'm afraid your mother is right--if anyone is to blame, I am. It was my responsibility to protect you. Unfortunately, I couldn't even help myself, so here we both are, orphans of the storm.

I'm glad to hear that you are finding some opportunities in the folk music field. You do want to be careful, though. I get the impression that real Communists do actually lurk behind the guitars and banjos of the "hootenanny" stage. Although, to be perfectly honest, I really know very little about the subject.

That seems to be my essential truth these days--I'm coming to realize that I know precious little about much of anything. When your country sucker punches you, it knocks you for a loop. I'm sure you feel that too, but in my case there is another quarter-century or so of accumulated beliefs and assumptions to eat, and it leaves a bitter taste in the mouth and a hollow pain in the belly.

(I had delusions of being a writer in my younger days, and you will notice the symptoms rising to the surface from time to time. I'll do my best to contain them.)

So far I have had no luck in one of my objectives in coming to Paris, which was to patch things up with my son Alden. We had a falling out a few years ago, when he accused me of being a prig and stuck in the 19th century. I took offense at the time, but I'm starting to suspect he may have even given me the benefit of a century or two.

I have been here for a week now, and I'm already beginning to feel at home here in a way I never did in Washington. I've made a friend in Jake Barnes, a veteran American journalist who is the Bureau Chief for the Paris Herald Tribune. He's easing my way into the expatriate community. He's a wonderful guy, big and bearded and full of life. And he's that rare bird, or rare in the circles I move in, a man with a conscience to match his intelligence. He actually sees the world in terms of right and wrong. You don't get much of that in Washington. Or even in Chicago, come to think of it.

He warned me off the expensive luxury of the Hotel George V, and arranged my move to a little dive on the Left Bank where I'm now in residence. It's an odd, narrow building that is said to date to the 16th century. I can well believe the plumbing hasn't changed since then, and the room is not much bigger than a closet, but there is a little wrought-iron balcony overlooking a pleasant little courtyard, and the price is right. The food is great, the wine is cheap, and the coffee is so good they have a different word for it over here, "café." But then they have a different word for everything. That's the French for you. And there's a bar called Harry's where they know how to make a martini that can make a man forget McCarthy.

Please do keep writing, and let me know how you're doing. I will feel much better about things if I know you've managed to land on your feet.

Yours Truly,

Nicholas Carraway

Ronnie Gilchrist
Martha Washington Hotel
New York City

March 19

Dear Mr. Carraway,

Thank you so much for responding to my letter. It means a lot to me that we can still be friends. And I just want to tell you that I LOVE the way you write, and if I could write like you do, that's what I'd want to do all the time.

Well, to make a long story short, Mr. Sheinbloom was calling about The Weavers! Have you ever heard of them? They're the folk music group Senator McCarthy was asking me about? They had that big hit song, "Goodnight Irene"? Anyway, he's an executive at Decca Records, and he manages them or something. He said he'd seen a kinny (sp.?) of me playing the banjo on "Snicklepoo" and he wanted me to come and audition for them!!!!! He said he'd pay my way to New York. So I decided to come, I mean I couldn't just sit around in Winnetka and listen to my mother.

Still, I was scared to death!!! Luckily I met this nice girl at the Martha Washington

Hotel for Women, where I'm staying. Her name is Jackie Susann and she wants to be a writer, and she gave me a pill to calm my nerves. I'm not sure what it was, but it really helped when I went in to see Mr. Sheinbloom. He told me that Mr. Seeger, who is one of the ones that started the group, might have to leave because of "trouble with the government," and they might need a replacement. I said "But I'm a girl!", and he just laughed and patted my knee and said he knew that--isn't that funny? And he wanted me to come in and meet the Weavers the next day!

You'll never guess who I got a call from that night!!!! Do you remember little Johnny Phillips, one of the Snicklekids on my very first show? He's a teenager now, and I guess he's in the mailroom or something at Decca Records. Anyway he'd heard about me auditioning for The Weavers, and he wanted me to show them some arrangements he'd been working on. He has all these ideas for four-part harmonies with two men and two girls. They're a little weird, I guess, but they sounded really good to me, or maybe it was just those pills Jackie gave me. Johnny was so sweet, he said I'd been sort of like a mama to him, and I was a bit embarrassed, but I told him we all need mamas and papas.

Anyway, when I got into Mr. Sheinbloom's office the next morning--that was this morning, it all just happened!--the Weavers were all there, except for Mr. Seeger. There was Mr. Lee Hays, who is this big teddy bear, so cute. And Ronnie Gilbert--she's the one who has a name that sounds like mine, that made Senator McCarthy so mixed up. And there's another one, they introduced me to him too, but I can't remember his name now. I guess I was too nervous. I tried to show them Johnny's arrangements, but Mr. Hays laughed and said they don't read music! He told me to just sing some songs that I knew. So I sang "John Jacob Jingleheimer Smith," and Mr. Hays joined in on the chorus, but the others didn't seem to like it much. Then I tried "Hi, Said the Little Leatherwinged Bat," and they all joined in on the "Howdy, dowdy" part! I thought it sounded really good, and Mr. Hays clapped when I played my banjo break!

Then I wanted to show them that I knew topical songs like they sang, so I did "The Ballad of Rodger Young." It's that wonderful sad song about a private in the infantry who "fought and died for the men he marched among." When I finished, Miss Gilbert kind of stared at me, and the other man said he was going to go get some fresh air, and Mr. Hays took Mr. Sheinbloom aside, and Mr. S. told me to go back to the hotel and he'd talk to me later. When he called he said it wasn't going to work out with The Weavers, but he's invited me to come up to his apartment this weekend to work with me on some new material. He's so nice!

But here's where I need your advice. He wants to bill me as "The Little Red Thrush." I'm worried it will remind people of Senator McCarthy's committee. What do you think? I can't go back to Winnetka.

Hoping all is well with you.

Your friend,

Ronnie Gilchrist

Roy M. Cohn, Esq.
Office of the Hon. Joseph McCarthy
Senate Office Building
Washington, DC

March 20, 1953

Davey,

It looks good for the Senator being able to keep you out of the draft. But we need to make sure that the world knows you're an important part of the Senator's crusade against the Communist Menace. I'm thinking of a fact-finding trip to Europe, which will give us high visibility (at least in the daytime). What facts, you ask? I don't know, but we'll find some!

Anyway, haven't I been promising you we'd take a vacation, just the two of us? The Europeans are a bunch of immoral pigs, but they do have some nice hotels. Don't forget to pack your purple briefs--you know the ones I mean. And that torn T-shirt, my little Stanley Kowalski! Ooh la la!

Love, Daddy

G. David Schine
Hay-Adams Hotel
Washington, DC

Sunday, March 22

Dear Christine,

Congratulations on the operation. But I have to admit I've got mixt feelings. You were such a cute boy.

"Daddy" is taking me to Europe! He says they're a bunch of immorral pigs over there--I can hardly wait! Not sure where we'll be--Germinny, I know, and Paris. Have you got any good French connections? I'd say let's get together but I don't think so. You know how jellus "Daddy" gets. (Anyway you're not my type any more, ha ha!)

Davey

PS. We're looking for REDS. Know any?

Ronnie Gilchrist
Martha Washington Hotel
New York City

March 22

Dear Mr. Carraway,

Just a quick note to tell you something I overheard last night at Mr. Sheinbloom's apartment when he was talking on the phone. That horrid little Mr. Cohn from the McCarthy Committee is going to Europe to look for Communists or something. Mr. Sheinbloom laughed and said, "He should be able to find some Communists in Europe, for God's sake. But if he really wanted a challenge, he'd go to Russia." I'm not sure where he actually will be going, but I did hear Mr. S mention Paris, where you are. I know it has nothing to do with you, but you be careful just the same. I don't like that Mr. Cohn!

Mr. S has arranged for me to open for Josh White at the Village Vanguard next week. I'm scared to death! But I've been working like mad, and I have learned some new songs, like "Last Night I Had the Strangest Dream," which is pretty and has a real message. Mr. S has found an apartment for me on MacDougal Street, which is right in

Greenwich Village, so I won't be at the Martha Washington any more. I'll miss Jackie and the other girls, but Mr. Sheinbloom says it will be more comfortable and private having a place of my own. Anyway, I'm feeling a little funny about the pills Jackie gives us. I really worry about Carole Landis and Barbara and especially Judy, sometimes they're so fun, and then all of a sudden they just seem to go so ... oh, I don't know, I guess I'm being silly, and I know Jackie says there's no harm in the pills, but maybe I'm better off moving. If you want to write me, the new address is Apartment C, 14½ MacDougal Street, New York 12, New York.

I am so nervous about where my career is going, and this whole "Little Red Thrush" thing . . . it is the last thing in the world I ever imagined myself doing, living in New York City and being a part of the whole folk music scene. But I don't know what else to do.

Anyway, you watch out for Mr. Cohn.

Your friend always,

Ronnie

Robert Cohn Associates
1853 M Street NW, Suite 830
Washington, DC

Tuesday, March 24th

Roy,

Attaboy, go get those lousy Commies! And listen, when you get to France, there's a son of a bitch in the press corps I'd like you to stick it to big time. Guy by the name of Jake Barnes, who I used to know way back when I was living in Paris. He's arrogant, thinks he's G-d's gift to women, and I'm damn sure he's a subversive.

I'm sending a note to my old friend Maurice Chevalier asking him to show you boys around when you're in Paris. I think you'll like Maurice--he's the sort of guy who's comfortable in any situation. He'll show you the real Paris, not the one the tourists and French people see.

Your uncle,

Robert

Robert Cohn Associates
1853 M Street NW, Suite 830
Washington, DC

Tuesday, March 24th

Mon cher Maurice,

My nephew Roy Cohn is coming to Paris on some business for Senator McCarthy. Maybe you've heard. He's traveling with a friend, David Schine. They're bookish boys, and will be spending a lot of time in libraries. I want you to see to it that they get out a bit. Show them a good time. My nephew's the possessive sort, and I suspect there's something more than meets the eye to his interest in his friend. I'd like to try a little experiment. Lay on the charm, especially with Schine. You know how to be charming, don't you, Maurice? I want to see how Roy reacts when he's hot under the collar.

My file on you is safe in my cabinet. I keep it under C, for Collaboration--I mean, for Chevalier. Thanks Maurice, I know I can count on you.

Robbie

Nicholas Carraway
Hotel Odeon
Paris

March 26, 1953

Dear Miss Gilchrist,

I apologize for taking so long to get back to you. Your earlier letter and this one reached me at the same time. European postal delivery can be charmingly quirky.
You ask for my advice about Mr. Sheinbloom's plan to bill you as the Little Red Thrush.

My advice is this: Get back to Winnetka on the next train! Beware of your friend Jackie and her pills, and Greenwich Village, and folk music, and above all Mr. Sheinbloom! You're a sweet young girl, and there are men who will take advantage of that.

I appreciate your warning to me to watch out for Roy Cohn. If he will leave me the Deux Magots, I am perfectly willing to give him the rest of Europe. The Deux Magots, I should tell you, is one of a cluster of cafés on St. Germain des Prés (others are called Flore and Lipp and such, but what can compare with the name Deux Magots!) where everyone seems to wind up sooner or later. It is a fascinating place for watching people.

My instincts about them are almost invariably wrong. I sat enthralled the other day watching a craggy fellow dressed in black velvet, smoking harsh yellow cigarettes, and scribbling in a notebook. He turned out to be an insurance salesman totting up actuarial charts. I paid no attention to a couple at the next table, a tall woman made taller by a bun of dark hair piled on top of her head, and a short, round-faced man blinking behind owlish spectacles. When my friend Jake Barnes arrived to join me, he identified them as the famous writers and existentialist philosophers, Simone de Beauvoir and Jean-Paul Sartre!

To my intense mortification, Barnes introduced me as "Nicholas Carraway, the American author." Mr. Sartre was very gracious, and asked me if I knew Nelson Algren, which seemed to annoy Miss de Beauvoir. She leaned over and whispered something to Mr. Sartre. Imagine my surprise when his face brightened and he said "Ah, Trimalchio in West Egg!" This is a man who is probably the most important thinker in Europe today, and he remembered my book! My "situation" seems to open more doors than it closes. McCarthy and his hysteria are more a joke over here than anything else and the intellectuals assure us patronizingly that they don't believe he represents "les vrais Americains." People are openly involved with Communism, but nobody gets too worked up about it, considering how much closer they are here to the grim specter of the Iron Curtain.

I am going to love the pace of Paris--the Deux Magots, the afternoon apéritifs with Jake, the sense that the world is both a larger and a more intimate place than I had ever imagined.

Your Friend,

Nick Carraway

Hotel de l'Odeon

Paris

Wednesday
Pour: M. Carraway
De la part de: M. Barnes

Carraway - what was I thinking, putting you in a place with no telephone? It's inconvenient as hell leaving these notes. Get your ass back to the George fucking Sank, where they've moved into the goddam 20th century! Anyway, meet me at the Deux Magots at 5:30 - I've got some hot poop. Guess who's heading this way with blood in his eye and lead in his pencil? Your old pal Roy Cohn, on a rampage through Europe with his playmate G. David Schine, in search of god knows what -

one minute they say they're ferreting out mismanagement and waste in the foreign information service, the next they're hunting for subversive literature in USIA libraries (does that ring a bell?), the next thing you know they'll be tracking down a really good liverwurst and a soft pair of bunny slippers. They landed in Frankfurt yesterday, and they've got Paris in their sights. The boys in the press rooms are agog. This could be the swellest thing to hit this town since they invented le strip tease. See you at dix-sept heures trente—or 5:30, whichever comes first—and we'll indulge in some honest drinking and treasonous ridicule of American indignitaries.

—Barnes

Hotel Majestic
1 Dong Khoi St
Saigon
Vietnam

27 March

Barnes,

Two-week holiday due me, and I'm on my way to Paris. You can fill me in on what kind of awful imperialist lunacy the bloody Yanks are up to these days. I swear, a few of them are even starting to filter into Saigon. Mostly, though, I just want to hit the nightspots and hear some good American jazz. I was hoping Philby could get over and join us for an old-fashioned pub crawl, but our old chum Kim has funked on us. Busy time at the Home Office, he claims, Lord knows what sort of bloody Yank fat to be pulled out of the fire this time. Thank the bloody heavens we British have never gone in for this imperialist nonsense, what?

Hope you appreciate the posh Majestic stationary. I cribbed some sheets while I was soaking up a pitcher of their gin rickeys, the best in Indo-China.

Regards,

Fowler

Hotel D'Angleterre
KONGENS NYTORV 34
COPENHAGEN, DENMARK

3 April

Dear Jake,

Tell me more about your Mr. Carraway. He interests me. You know I've always been attracted to men of your generation--dare I say, without risking bruised feelings, "older men"? Of course, I wouldn't ever lump you in with any generalization. You're my Jake, and always will be.

This will amuse you. A boy I used to know, Davey Schine, dropped by to see me here in Copenhagen. Does the name ring a bell? He's on a rampage through Europe with his friend Roy Cohn, Joe McCarthy's hatchet man. ("Daddy," Davey calls Roy--sweet, isn't it?) Perhaps you've run into them? Apparently they're kicking up quite a ruckus in your neck of the woods.

I met Davey and Roy through Clyde Tolson and his friend, He Who Must Not Be Named, back when I was exploring the conventionally unconventional avenues of sexuality. Davey's a nice boy, maybe a little too full of uncritical enthusiasm for his own good. It's a quality that's taken him down some peculiar alleys. He's not the brightest sparkler in the packet, but he listens well, and he's mentioned a few rather startling tidbits that may have rolled off the pillow, and that could be classified as Hot International Stuff. (It all has to do with that Mossadegh fellow you were writing about recently.) I have impressed upon Dear Davey that he is not to talk about these things with anybody but his Uncle George--excuse me, his Aunt Christine--but to tell me everything!

I will discreetly pass it all along to you, my darling newshound, when I see you in Paris next week.

Much love,
C.

Hotel de l'Odeon

Paris

Mr. Alden Carraway
c/o American Consulate
Kathmandu, Nepal

April 4

Dear Alden,

I have no idea whether this letter will find you. If it does, it's a better man than I. I'm writing this from Paris, where I came at least in part to find you, and seem to have missed you by a matter of days. The other part of my visit, I guess, was to try to find myself, as I suppose you're doing in your monastery or ashram.

It's amazing the things you can see when you step back a few paces. Some of the picture is not very pretty. There are parts of it that make me despair; other parts fill me with an enormous patriotic pride. I have always imagined myself a "good American"; but I think I'm only just beginning to understand what that means.

I saw Chaplin's "Limelight" last night on the Champs-Élysées with Jake Barnes, who's taken me under his wing since I arrived in Paris. He has wonderful things to say about you, which makes me very proud. Anyway, it was a marvelous movie. One of my first official acts in Washington was to sign off on a recommendation to Attorney General Brownell that Chaplin's expulsion from the United States not be reviewed. I thought it made sense from that side of the Atlantic. Now I wonder. America is a great country, Alden, the greatest experiment in liberty the world has ever seen. Whether an artist's views are the same as mine or Dorothy Kilgallen's or Joe McCarthy's, we ought perhaps to have room for their expression. In fact, I'm beginning to think we must make that room, if we are to survive.

I'm so sorry to have missed you here in Paris, Alden. I have your general whereabouts from Jake. Don't blame him for telling me where you are. There was and is a lot I have to say to you about you and me and the missed opportunities and the lost years. I have a feeling you and I can bridge those gaps, but we'll need to sit down together for a few long afternoons. Please write and let me know how you're doing. I am longing to see you.

Your loving father

Jacob Barnes
Paris Herald Tribune
38, rue de Berri
Paris 16, France

April 5th, or thereabouts

Fowler,

Well, get your gin-soaked ass over here! How the hell are you? How the hell have you been? If you see any Americans in Saigon, shoot them. With my permission. That's the only goddam language they understand. It'll be damn good to see you. Fuck Philby, it's his loss. Bud Powell is playing at Le Bar Negre--not that sort of watered-down oompah music you Brits call jazz, but something damn honest and true. The kind of thing you need to hear, before you jump to too many conclusions about America.

I'll introduce you to my new pal Nick Carraway. You may remember--I sent you his novel years ago, the one about the gangster who falls in love with the rich dame. Since he's been here he's been coming in for a good dose of your damn old-Europe Yank-bashing, which is doing him some good. The Europeans are sore as hell over Chaplin, and I think a few scales are beginning to drop from Carraway's eyes. He still has too many illusions about America, and we can't cure what's wrong with America with illusions. Damn fine writer though, and a good man, though he can't always hold his liquor.

Don't try to get him to any of your favorite bordels, although he could use it. He's tied up like a knot below the belt. Anyway, he's got this idea his wee-wee is too small. Told me the other night when he was tight. Tells everybody when he's tight, I hear. He'll tell you if you get him tight.

Just as glad Philby won't be here. I don't want to get in the middle of that. Spender doesn't trust him worth a damn, but he's been sucking up to Kristol like nobody's business, and they've gotten to be thick as thieves.

Anyway, we'll have entertainment. McCarthy's Two Stooges, Cohn and Schine, hit town tonight, fresh from a boffo engagement in Frankfurt. You must have read a word or two about it, even out there in the fucking Orient. So come!

Yr. loyal partner in depravity,

Barnes

Apartment C
14½ MacDougal Street
New York

April 5, 1953

Dear Mr. Carraway,

That sounds so formal, now that we've been writing each other back and forth like this, and you're not married anymore. (Oh, goodness--I don't know what I meant by that!) I remember a lot of the people on the show used to call you Nick, and I always called you Mr. Carraway, and one of the Snicklekids--do you remember Mary Richards?--used to tease me about it. She said when she grew up, she wasn't going to let anyone push her around, and she would always call her boss by his first name. Anyway, I hope I'm not sounding too much like a small-town girl from the Midwest. I'm trying to be a real New Yorker now. I wear black leotards and peasant blouses and eye makeup, just like all the other kids who come out to Washington Square Park on Sunday to sing folk music. This week a few people even recognized me. Some of them even took my picture--a couple of men in suits and snap-brim hats and dark glasses--I guess they were tourists, they didn't look like the Greenwich Village types.

But you really are my best friend, you know. Whenever something important happens to me, or I find myself really thinking deeply about something (not that I'm saying my thoughts are so terribly deep or anything), I always wish you were here. New York can be a lonely town, and I sometimes think how good it would be to have a shoulder to cry on, and someone to say, there, there, Ronnie, you're going to be all right.

Oh, I know I'm being silly. I hope you won't think I'm just a silly girl and stop writing to me altogether.

Your friend always,

Ronnie

Hotel George V

31 Avenue George V
Paris 8eme
France

Roy Cohn
Suite 7A

April 7

Dear Uncle Robert,

Thanks for your note of encouragement. That's right, you lived in Paris for a few years in your reckless youth, didn't you? When you were writing your pinko novels. Don't worry, your books are safe!

Davey and I have been having a ball on this trip. You wouldn't believe the European press. They're really spazzing out over us, but they're dumb enough to jerk around--it's like throwing a bone for a dumb dog and you throw it over the fence and the dog smashes into the fence chasing it. Really funny! Davey wrote a poem I think you'll like. Here it is:

> Europe is a fucking whore
> Parlay-voo francais
> Why we saved 'em in the war

Is more than I can say
The Frenchies kissed our G.I. ass
Voulay-voo Paree
Now they give us frogs and gas,
The men are slow, the girls are fast,
Well I for one will take a pass
Who gives a fart? Not me!

Is this a talented kid or what? I made him sign it and then I grabbed it and posted it at the concierge's desk. Davey went bananas! He chased me through the lobby of the Georges V trying to swat me with a rolled-up magazine! I was yelling "Commie swine" and ducking for cover. It was a hoot! The snooty hotel manager tried to put a damper on us, but I dropped Senator McCarthy's name and he left us alone. What a dork!

Speaking of people who seem to think a lot of themselves, your pal Barnes showed up at the press conference we had the day we got here. You're right, he's an arrogant sonofabitch. He asked what kind of books we were trying to weed out of the USIA libraries. I said, "What kind of books do you think, Mr. Barnes?" He said, "If I were fighting communism, I don't think I'd give people any books at all." I'm not sure what he meant by that, but I'm going to pass his name along to our staff.

I can see why you liked Paris. There's something going on every minute here--no bull!!!! Maurice is taking us to a nightclub tonight--a "boat," they call them here. I'll keep you posted when I can grab a moment to write. We'll be here a few more days, and then heading home to file a report for the Senator.

Love to Aunt Frances.

Roy

Submission to the Herald Tribune
Music Review
Francis Paudras

April 7, 1953

Attn: M. Barnes

PARIS--The great American pianist Bud Powell played what turned out to be two solo sets at Le Bar Negre last night. Hampered at first by a sluggish rhythm section of Parisian locals, M. Powell soon left them behind. First the drummer, then the bass player trailed off, and stood watching M. Powell in disbelief. They did not return to the bandstand for the second set.

Powell took familiar standards like "Tea for Two" and newer bebop compositions like "Ornithology," and led them through a series of runs up and down the keyboard, in and out of time and melody, crashing up against chords that seemed to have positioned themselves at unexpected junctions around hairpin turns, then emerging unscathed on the other side, but for a few distinguishing wisps plucked from the chord, much like other American geniuses such as les Keystone Cops or Messrs. Abbott and Costello driving their flivvers into a barn and coming out the other side. There is no hayseed on M. Powell, but he exhibits the same consummate skill and timing masked as utter recklessness.

On the night this reporter ventured out to review M. Powell's performance, the audience included Messrs. Roy Cohn and G. David Schine, the associates of the American Senator Joseph McCarthy, at a table with the Vichy collaborator Maurice Chevalier. They left during the first set, as M. Powell was negotiating a breathtaking passage of "You Brought a New Kind of Love to Me." At another table, nearer the bandstand, was a group that included M. Jacob Barnes, managing editor of the Paris Herald Tribune, M. Thomas Fowler, Asian correspondent of the Times of London, M. Nicholas Carraway, an American novelist, and Mlle. Christine Jorgensen, best known for her recent medical procedure in Copenhagen.

At the end of the second set, M. Powell joined this latter group, and it was then that the evening took a bizarre and very nearly a tragic turn. After a round of drinks, M. Powell's behavior began to change. He seemed to take offense at a remark by M. Carraway. Then, without warning, he leaped up from his chair, grabbed the bottle, and smashed it against the table, cutting his hand in the process. The white tablecloth was quickly drenched in blood.

M. Barnes took M. Powell by the arm and calmed him, guiding him to the next table where he deftly removed the sliver of glass from M. Powell's hand. All this time he was speaking quietly, revealing a surprising knowledge of the Harlem of M. Powell's boyhood. The great musician visibly relaxed as they discussed shops and street corners and small nightclubs, and musicians like Willie "The Lion" Smith and James P. Johnson. Their conversation turned to Kansas City, where M. Barnes was raised. M. Powell's eyes lit up. "Did you know Lester Young and Count Basie?" he asked. "Did you hear Bird play back in KC?"

"I left Kansas City before the war," M. Barnes answered. "Before the great jazz clubs opened. But I did hear Scott Joplin play in Sedalia, when I was a kid. His music had dignity and truth, the truth from which all music must start. Your playing has that truth, too. I visited New York a number of times in the Thirties. But then the war started, and I did not leave Europe in those years. I heard stories, though, about the after-hours sessions at Minton's Playhouse, and the greatness of Thelonious Monk."

M. Powell's eyes grew dim, and he seemed to be somewhere else. "Minton's," he said. "I was there, you know, the night they raided the place. They went after Monk. They came after him with clubs, and they put the cuffs on him."

"I heard about that," M. Barnes said. "You wouldn't let the cops take him. You told them, 'You don't know what you're doing. You're mistreating the greatest musician in the world!'"

"That's what they say," M. Powell said. "I don't remember nothing."

"They hit you," M. Barnes said. "They clubbed you on the head with a nightstick."

"Me," M. Powell said proudly. "Not Monk. Me. I stopped them from hitting Monk. I know, because when I woke up, we were in a cell together, and Monk was all right. They arrested the greatest musician in the world, but they didn't hit him. Me. Not Monk."

There are rumors that M. Powell suffers from nervous disorders, as a result of that blow. It is apparent, however, that his mistreatment at the hands of the iniquitous American justice system has not affected his genius.

--Francis Paudras

Paudras - stick to the music, and cut out all the other crap. What is this, a music review or a soap opera? If it's a news story, you buried the lead. — Barnes

Hotel de l'Odeon

Paris

April 7, 1953

Dear Ronnie,

I'm afraid that I have a lot to learn about life, and am just beginning to find out how much. Earlier tonight Barnes took me out to a bistro to hear some jazz. At least Barnes said it was going to be jazz, but it's a far cry from what my generation danced to, in those halcyon days we called the Jazz Age. Afterward, the pianist--an American Negro named Powell--came over to our table, and I managed to insult him. I was trying to be friendly, and I said, "Is that what you hepcats nowadays call beep-bop? Like that Thelonious Monkey and all those other strange musicians who wear those outlandish sunglasses and goatees?" I realized even as I was saying it that I was making a total ass of myself and trying to pretend to know something I know nothing about, but I wasn't prepared for what followed.

He came at me, with intent to kill. He smashed a bottle and brandished it in my face, his hand bloody from the flying glass. It was truly frightening. But Barnes stepped in between us, and I don't know how he did it, but without raising his voice or using any physical force, he gently steered Mr. Powell away. He sat him down at a nearby table, and talked to him for maybe half an hour. Ronnie, he was marvelous!

After that, Mr. Powell and I shook hands and made up. I apologized, and he patted my shoulder and said, "I get crazy sometimes, man." We walked him back to his hotel, to see that he arrived safely--and to make sure that he didn't drink any more--and I found myself looking at his eyes, deeply troubled and profoundly calm at the same time, and wishing I could talk to him the way Barnes can. My experiences are starting to seem awfully shallow to me. There's tragedy in that Negro's eyes, and I suspect that behind every tragedy there's a hero.

Your devoted friend,

Nick

Hotel Danemark

21, Rue Vavin

Paris 6e, France

April 8

Dear Helen,

An added surprise on my Paris trip. You'll have read about the notorious Christine Jorgensen--the American soldier who recently went from a him to a her? It turns out she's a close pal of Barnes's, and she joined us on our Paris pub crawl (incognito, to evade my journalistic brethren--or perhaps they stayed away out of deference to Barnes). She turns out to be a very attractive woman--the photographs don't do her justice. And quite feminine ... no, womanly might be a better word. She has a maturity about her that one does not always encounter in one so young, and rarely if ever in Americans.

Speaking of which, Barnes is top drawer. Hard to believe he's a Yank. I saw him defuse a situation between an American writer named Carraway and a nigger piano player last night. I would have simply tried to get us all out of there, but Barnes sat down and talked to the fellow. Had him telling us his life story. Carraway, Miss

Jorgensen and I listened spellbound. The four of us ended the evening by seeing the nigger chap home to a small flat in the 5th.

Not sure what to make of this Carraway--mostly, I believe, because he's not sure what to make of himself. I believe he's someone who has always lived through others. Perhaps that's what made him such a good novelist, although he's only written one book. Barnes sent it to me years ago--I believe he's sent it to everyone he knows --and I understood why he liked it, but I'm afraid it was too American for me. At any rate, Barnes has quite taken him under his wing.

Perhaps one had to have lived through what Barnes and Carraway and his man Gatsby lived through in their war. Barnes is fond of saying "one of us," a phrase which he tinges, however, with irony. He includes me when he says it, for better or for worse, but I don't belong. There's something that always set that generation apart. Certainly my crowd at Oxford thought so. We never got over being the generation that didn't go to war. Which meant, of course, that we also were not the generation that didn't come back. And that often seemed to be the hardest part. Barnes represents something to us, and that may be part of the reason he is held in such high regard. That, and of course the fact that he's a damned good journalist and a damned good drinker.

Spender and Auden and Isherwood, when they weren't talking about revolution, were talking about the coming war. They started anticipating it by about 1922, I'd say. I suppose anything was better than looking back at the classes just before us at Oxford, which essentially didn't exist. It was eerie.

Well, the coming war came, did it not? And I can't say we're the better for it. I don't know that I like being "one of us." I'm tired of having to choose up sides, and I suspect many of my friends feel the same way. "Taking sides" these days means either being for or against America, and both positions grow more and more untenable. Still, it must be very strange for those veterans of what they used to call The Great War, to suddenly no longer be numbered among the happy few.

Now, about that divorce ...

Sincerely yours,

Thomas

Hotel D'Angleterre
KONGENS NYTORV 34
COPENHAGEN, DENMARK

9 April

Dear Jake,

Thanks for the evening. Paris was wonderful.

How have you stayed away from America for so long? Were you trying to prove something? To yourself? Because you're American to the core, darling, and you love the damn country. Always have, always will. I know, because I don't.

I don't hate America. It's like my male equipment. Painful to admit, even to myself, that I didn't need it, because everyone said it was the greatest thing in the world. But easy to shed, once I'd made up my mind. I don't hate men (at all), but I hated myself, being a man, and I'm still learning to separate myself from that self-hatred. But the physical parts themselves ... it's strange but true. They're gone and forgotten. No nostalgic backward glances, no regrets.

So I know what it's like to leave something and not miss it. And if that was how you were when you talked about America, I'd recognize it in you. But you're not like that. Something else is inside you.

And I like it, you old bear.

Love,
C

Dr. Christian Hamburger
Director of Special Surgery
Royal Hospital
Copenhagen, Denmark

April 9, 1953

Dear Mr. Barnes,

Miss Christine Jorgensen has related to me your correspondence with her regarding your condition.

Without a physical examination, of course, it would be impossible for me to venture an informed evaluation of your candidacy for the kind of procedure we can offer here. However, I must say that on the basis of Miss Jorgensen's descriptions, I am intrigued by the possibilities. Medical science has made enormous strides in the decades since you suffered your disability, and I flatter myself that here at the clinic we have been at the forefront--dare I say the cutting edge?--of the technology from which you might hope to benefit.

Copenhagen is a day's journey from Paris. While it would be unprofessional of me to dangle expectations, I am optimistic enough to encourage you to make the trip.

Very Truly Yours,

Dr. Christian Hamburger
Director of Special Surgery

(ENCRYPTED AND DECODED)
(4/9)
FROM: ALLEN DULLES
TO: IRVING KRISTOL

CAN'T ALLOW STRONG FIGURE LIKE DEGAULLE TO CONSOLIDATE POWER IN FRANCE. OPERATION DESERT RAT READY TO ROLL, AND THAT'S OUR OUT-OF-TOWN TRYOUT, THE NEW HAVEN OF OUR STRATEGY. IF IT'S A HIT, OPERATION ELBA OUR BROADWAY OPENING. DOMINO THEORY. IF IT PLAYS IN IRAN, NO REASON IT WON'T WORK IN FRANCE. OPERATION ELBA SWINGS INTO GEAR. EUROPE ROLLS OVER LIKE CIRCUS POODLE. NEED TO KEEP FRANCE WEAK AND CONFUSED.
DULLES

(ENCRYPTED AND DECODED)
(4/9)
FROM: ALLEN DULLES
TO: ROBERT COHN

DO YOU REALLY HAVE THAT NEPHEW OF YOURS UNDER CONTROL? HAVE DOUBTS ABOUT THE WISDOM OF THIS STRATEGY.

DULLES

(ENCRYPTED AND DECODED)
(4/9)
FROM: IRVING KRISTOL
TO: ALLEN DULLES

I HAVE A PLAN FOR FRANCE. WE'RE BUILDING UP ONE OF THEIR POLITICIAN-OF-THE-MONTH-CLUB CIPHERS, PIERRE MENDES-FRANCE, TO GIVE THE ILLUSION HE'S A FIGURE OF STRENGTH. BUT WE'RE SECRETLY INDOCTRINATING HIM TO BELIEVE THAT WINE IS SAPPING THE FRENCH MORAL FIBER. WHEN THE MOMENT IS RIGHT, WE'LL HAVE HIM PHOTOGRAPHED DRINKING MILK--THEN THE WHOLE GOVERNMENT SHOULD COLLAPSE AGAIN.

KRISTOL

(ENCRYPTED AND DECODED)
(4/9)
FROM: ALLEN DULLES
TO: IRVING KRISTOL

BRILLIANT. YOU'VE GOT A FUTURE AS A TROUBLEMAKER, KRISTOL. NOW ABOUT THE COHN-SCHINE JUNKET. NOT COMFORTABLE WITH LEAVING THIS IN CARRAWAY'S HANDS.

DULLES

(ENCRYPTED AND DECODED)
(4/9)
FROM: ROBERT COHN
TO: ALLEN DULLES

I HAVE A PLAN FOR ROY. OF COURSE THAT FAGGOT NEPHEW OF MINE WILL FUCK THINGS UP. WE TURN IT TO OUR ADVANTAGE. YOU NEED TO BE MORE CREATIVE IN YOUR THINKING, DULLES. SEMPER PARATUS. REMIND ME SOME TIME TO TELL YOU ABOUT MY THEORY OF USING DIFFERENT SIDES OF YOUR BRAIN.

COHN

(ENCRYPTED AND DECODED)
(4/9)
FROM: ALLEN DULLES
TO: ROBERT COHN

THIS IS A GOVERNMENT SERVICE. PLEASE WATCH YOUR LANGUAGE. DO NOTHING WITHOUT CLEARING WITH ME.

DULLES

(ENCRYPTED AND DECODED)
(4/9)
FROM: IRVING KRISTOL
TO: ALLEN DULLES

YOU KNOW HOW ROBERT COHN IS. IF HE ENTERS THE PICTURE, WE NEED TO THROW ALL OUR PLANS OUT THE WINDOW. BUT WE'VE IMPROVISED BEFORE, WE CAN DO IT AGAIN. MEANWHILE, IF WE WANT TO INCLUDE BARNES IN THE PICTURE, WE NEED TO BRING HIM INTO FOCUS SOON. THE COHNS APPEAR TO HAVE A GRUDGE AGAINST HIM. BARNES AND CARRAWAY HAVE BECOME THICK. I'D SAY IT'S TIME TO MOVE THE CARRAWAY PAWN FORWARD, OPEN UP THAT GAMBIT. OF COURSE, THIS COULD MEAN THROWING YOUR MAN TO THE WOLVES, IF WE GO TO IMPROVISATION MODE. PROBLEMS WITH THAT?

KRISTOL

(ENCRYPTED AND DECODED)
(4/9)
FROM: ALLEN DULLES
TO: IRVING KRISTOL

DON'T WASTE WORDS. THESE CABLES COME FROM OUR BUDGET. CAN THROW CARRAWAY TO WOLVES IF NEED BE. BARNES TOO?

DULLES

(ENCRYPTED AND DECODED)
(4/9)
FROM: ROBERT COHN
TO: ALLEN DULLES

ALLIE--DON'T WORRY ABOUT A THING. TRUST ME.

ROBBIE

(ENCRYPTED AND DECODED)
(4/9)
FROM: IRVING KRISTOL
TO: ALLEN DULLES

I'M AN INTELLECTUAL, REMEMBER? TO ME, THIS IS BEING CONCISE. NO PROBLEM IN THROWING BARNES TO THE WOLVES. IF WE CAN USE HIM, ALL TO THE GOOD. BUT I'VE BEEN TALKING TO PHILBY, AND HE TELLS ME THERE'S SCUTTLEBUTT OVER IN MI-6 ABOUT ENCOUNTER HAVING TIES TO THE COMPANY. I'M THINKING IF COHN ENDS UP MAKING BARNES THE SCAPEGOAT, WE CAN DISTRACT ATTENTION AWAY FROM CERTAIN OTHER ENCOUNTER EDITORS, SUCH AS YOUR HUMBLE SERVANT.

KRISTOL

Apartment C
14½ MacDougal Street
New York

April 9, 1953

Dear ... Nick ... ?

There, I said it. Do I seem like a forward, brassy girl? I hope not. It sounds strange ... but nice.

I guess you did make a mistake with Mr. Powell about Mr. Monk, but how could you know? I wouldn't have, either, just a few days ago.

The thing about Mr. Monk is, he's a genius and he's been so terribly mistreated that his friends feel really protective of him. I found that out when a couple of Mr. Sheinbloom's friends (a very gentlemanly Turkish man named Ahmet Ertegun, and his partner, a real Noo Yawker named Jerry Wexler) took me to a club in Greenwich Village where they said Thelonious Monk would be playing. It was a secret, because they couldn't advertise it, because Monk--that's what they call him, Monk--do I sound like a sophisticated New Yorker?--isn't allowed to play in any clubs in New York. Mr. Wexler told me why. It's because jazz is a blow for freedom, and The Establishment wants to wipe out freedom. So Monk was arrested on some trumped-up charge, and now he can't get a cabaret card, which means now he can't play his music anywhere in New York, and that's about the most unfair thing I ever heard, next to what happened to you.

Anyway, the musicians were already playing when we got there, and suddenly there was a hush over the whole room, and I looked up, and the kitchen door opened, and out walked Monk. He has an aura about him that makes you tingle. He started playing, and at first nothing seemed to fit. All these notes--they weren't exactly chords, they were more like jammed together as if he was squeezing them into a ball in his fist instead of playing them. But then I started to hear them differently, and suddenly bit by bit they started to come together, as if these were the harmonies of the angels from the heaven of whatever strange world it was that Monk lives in, and all I could think was, "I wish I could sing that." Sometimes I get so tired of "Michael, Row the Boat Ashore."

Then somebody yelled out "Cops!" and the next thing I knew, they were hurrying Monk off the bandstand and out the kitchen door again, and suddenly four policemen came running in, swinging nightsticks. It was scary! They wouldn't let any of us leave until they'd taken everyone's name and address down.

So I guess that's why Mr. Powell acted so odd. I know it didn't really have anything to do with you. It's Monk--people get fierce about him. You should have seen how they took care of him that night with the police. I never saw anything like it.

Funny, I always thought of policemen as our friends. But then, I always thought of our government as good people, protecting us from the Communists. But so many things are happening to me. In many ways, I'm not the girl you knew. I hope you'd still like me. I hope you'd like me better. I feel like I'm not a girl anymore, I'm a woman.

Your special friend,

Ronnie

Apartment C
14½ MacDougal Street
New York

April 9, 1953

Dear Jackie,

Hi, girl--surprised to hear from me? How are things at the Martha Washington? Still breaking all the rules--and getting away with it??? Ha ha.

I need you to tell me something ... I hope I haven't made a terrible mistake. I really, really, really hope, because I wrote the letter a few days ago, and I already sent it off, and then I started thinking about ... well ... if there's a guy you think maybe you really like more than anyone else in the world, and he's a long way away, like maybe Paris, France, and you wrote him a letter, and in it you said, "I'm not a girl anymore ... I'm a woman," would he get the wrong idea?

Can you keep a secret? I went to this party with Mr. Sheinbloom at his friend Jerry Wexler's, who owns a record company. The Weavers were there (except Mr. Seeger), and Burl Ives, and we were going to hear this wonderful new blind singer and piano player that Mr. Wexler's label has just signed.

He was "real" cool! And you know what? He sang this one song where he needed some girl singers in the background, and Jerry told me to get up with these two Negro girls named Ruth and Lavern. I think they were the best singers I ever heard, and I had no business singing with them, but they were awful nice to me, and told me to keep at it.

Afterward this young guy named Chuck came up to me. He's a singer and a songwriter from St. Louis, he's here trying to get a recording contract, and he told me he really liked the way I sang, and the way I looked. He couldn't get over my eye makeup, and I told him it was just Maybelline, that all the girls down in Greenwich Village wear lots of eye makeup, to look more sophisticated. I told him back in my school days in Winnetka, I thought the height of being grownup was to wear tight dresses and lipstick, and high-heeled shoes, but that all seemed so teenage now.

Anyway, the way he kept looking at me when we were talking, it made my skin go all goose-bumpy, and I could tell he wanted to, you know ...

But just then there was a big commotion and Mr. Sheinbloom had gone all purple and couldn't breathe, and he was saying "The cat! The cat!" Mr. Wexler's cat had gotten out of the bedroom and jumped in his lap and Mr. Sheinbloom is deathly allergic, and I had to take him home, so I didn't get to see Chuck again. But that other guy from the Weavers, whose name I can never remember, drove us, and after we got Mr. Sheinbloom to bed he insisted on driving me home.

And I don't know, Jackie, maybe it was that I was still so hot and bothered or whatever from being with Chuck, but next thing I knew ... well ... you know that thing I was, that I didn't want to be? Well I'm not anymore.

The worst of it is, I still can't think of his name! They say a girl never forgets her first. I guess I'll never remember.

Your friend,

Ronnie

PS. Do you think it was OK? The letter, I mean?

Robert Cohn Associates
1853 M Street NW, Suite 830
Washington, DC

April 10

Dear Roy,

I had breakfast up on the hill with your boss this morning. McCarthy is as proud of you as if you were his nephew. Believe me, he's following the headlines from your trip like they were box scores from the Washington Senators.

Over coffee, he looked a little down, and for a moment I thought I sensed a little disappointment that there hadn't been anything really climactic. "A capper," he said, dabbing distractedly at a spot of egg yolk on his tie. "There's gotta be a capper!"

But then he looked up at me, and a big grin spread across his face. "He'll do it," he said. "The kid's got imagination. The kid's got balls! You watch, Cohn--that nephew of yours'll come up with something spectacular!"

I tell you, Roy, watching that smile spread across that five o'clock shadow (this is morning, mind you) it was like watching the sun break through storm clouds over a Wisconsin swamp. That man thinks a lot of you. He's expecting something big.

I know you won't let him down.

Your proud uncle,

Robert

Jacqueline Susann
Martha Washington Hotel
New York City

April 10, 1953

Ronnie,

Don't worry, kiddo. Men are all alike. If a man likes you that way, he suspects you with every man who ever lived, but he doesn't really think you'd ever do it with anyone except him. So don't worry, it never hurts to keep 'em guessing.

So ... little Ronnnnieeeeee!!!!!!!!! Woo woo!!!! But here's a word of advice from a babe who's fallen off a few cabbage trucks in her day. You can have a fling or two, but when you get ready for the One That Counts, here are your Aunt Jackie's Three Rules for Choosing a Man.

Rule Number One: Think Older.

Rule Number Two: Think Jewish.

So far, your friend Wexler sounds he's got potential, but don't ever forget Rule Number Three:

Think Broadway.

All that jazzy-jazz and folky-folk stuff will never get you anywhere. This is New York, kiddo.

Love and kisses,

Jackie

FROM THE DESK OF:

ALLEN DULLES

By Diplomatic Pouch
April 10, 1953

Carraway,

Sorry to have had to leave you out in the cold through all this. I trust in your heart of hearts you never doubted that I, and the Agency, were behind you, but for obvious reasons it was important that this situation be allowed to unfold in a way that would arouse no suspicion whatsoever.

Mind you, the McCarthy development was not one that we put into play, but here at the Company I've encouraged a tradition of seat-of-the-pants adapting to circumstances that I learned from my mentor, Wild Bill Donovan. So when the junior senator gave us a way to position you deep under cover where you could do the most good, it was a gift we had to seize. I apologize if it caused any difficulties for you personally. You can't make sausage without letting a little blood.

I've kept a close eye on you. Believe me when I say we were never going to let anything bad happen to you. There were moments when we were on the verge of stepping in, but instead we watched with gratified fascination as your instincts took you in exactly the right direction. You're good, Carraway. You're damned good. Someday, when this is all over and the world is safe, you and I need to sit down with a bottle of bourbon and talk about what you knew, and how you managed it.

The pieces are moving into place. The time is now.

Bring in Barnes.

Dulles

Lady Brett Ashley

Grand Hotel
New Delhi

April 10

Dear Jake,

Bulletin from the spirit world: the spirit was willing, but the flesh was stronger. It seems you can't teach an old cat new tricks.

Not strictly true, darling. The Maharishi taught me a trick or two I would never have dreamed possible. A nifty little number called tantric sex. Orgasms composed of two parts butterfly wing and five parts diesel locomotive. And I'm not talking about the Brighton local, darling, I'm talking about the Orient Express.

Oh, I know you hate it when I tell you these things. But you love it, too. Given our rotten damned circumstances, it's the closest we've got to intimacy, isn't it? And you've always been the only one I could talk to. Even five thousand miles away, you're still the man I want to run to whenever I've been naughty. Because no matter whom

I've been naughty with, Jake darling, it's really always you. Like that shah from the Middle East I was seeing just before I left Paris. Always told him I was in love with you. True, too.

I've left the ashram. The Maharishi was sweet, he begged me to stay, but you know, I'm just not much of a one-guru gal. And truth be told, darling, at my age you don't want to lie still too long. It's harder to spot the wrinkles on a moving target. The Maharishi is surrounded by all those guileless, willing twenty-three-year-old heiresses with firm titties and legs like baguettes. He was sweet, he offered to send them all away if I'd only stay another week, but you don't live a half a century as a temptress without picking up a few practical bits of wisdom.

So I'm down, but not out. Down from the mountaintop, that is. I'm in New Delhi, making up my mind which way to let the wind blow me next. I'd love to come back to Paris. I miss you, you know? But it's not going to happen right away.

I met a young chap at the monastery. Alden. Young and vigorous and very American, and I guess he reminds me of you--or what you would have been, darling, if it hadn't been for rotten luck and that damned war. Remember Pedro Romero, the bullfighter? Sort of like that, only very American, and of course I never let Alden see me in good light. Not that there's any good light at the monastery. I suspect he'll be leaving there soon. I'm afraid it turned out that the celibate life wasn't for him, either. I'm afraid he's quite smitten with me.

So I'll play this one out a little farther, till my whiskers tell me the magic's wearing thin, and then I'll jump off the roof before I get pushed. One of these days you'll hear me scratching at your door again, with a tale or two to tell. Have a bowl of warm milk standing by.

Oh Jake, we could have had such a damned good time together!

Love Always,

Brett

Atlantic Records

Interoffice Memo

Date: April 10

From: Wexler
To: A. Ertegun

Ahmet--

Let's keep an eye on this girl. She has nice tits, which is reason enough, but there's more. You heard her the other night singing backup for Ray, which is in a way easy, because Ray's doing shit no one ever did before, so there's no right or wrong way to do it, which is something you wouldn't necessarily think about, because the other half of it is so obvious--it's difficult as all fuck, because no one ever did it before.

But the kid got up there with Ruthie and LaVern, and hung in there. She mostly hit all the right notes, which is too bad. But every now and then she took a chance, and once--maybe twice--she found something.

Right now she's singing that hootenanny shit, and I don't want to push her too hard into changing. She needs some time to develop. She's spent too much fucking time singing nursery rhymes to kiddies, and you can tell. She's got an innocence about her that I hope she never loses completely, but she'll grow up fast enough in New York. Especially if she spends much time with guys like that kid-shtupper Sheinbloom.

She's learning the ropes, but she's not doing anything that challenges her musically, and pretty soon she's going to realize that. I think she could be another fucking Chris Connor.

What did you think of the Berry kid? I say pass on him. He's got his own style, and it ain't never gonna be our style. That hillbilly stuff may play in the Midwest. But this is fucking New York.

Jerry

Maurice Chevalier

April 10

Mon cher Cohn,
I have been entertaining your nephew and his friend (particularly the friend) according to your instructions. Enclosed you will find an account of expenses. Ca coute cher, mon vieux. David aime bien le champagne.

Maurice

4/11/53

FROM: ROY COHN
HOTEL GEORGE V
PARIS

TO: ROBERT COHN
WASHINGTON DC

UNCLE ROBERT
TELL MCCARTHY AND DULLES DONT WORRY STOP
WORKING ON NEAT PLAN FOR CARRAWAY AND BARNES
STOP DAVEY SPENDING TOO MUCH TIME WITH
DEGENERATE FRENCH STOP CHEVALIER GOING TO
HIS HEAD STOP SICK OF EUROPE STOP NO BULL

ROY

FROM THE DESK OF:

ROBERT COHN

BY MESSENGER
April 11

Hey Allie,

Had a cable from Roy. He says he's working on a "neat plan." I'll try to get details. Knowing my idiot nephew it could be entertaining, or it could be disastrous. Very likely both. In any case, we should be able to use it and still have complete deniability. We want things unsettled in France, right?

Robbie

FROM THE DESK OF:

ALLEN DULLES

By special courier

4/11

Cohn,

Don't let him do anything till I approve it.

Dulles

FROM THE DESK OF:

ROBERT COHN

BY MESSENGER

April 11

Allie-boy

Loosen up! Seat-of-the-pants, remember?

Robbie

Hotel de l'Odeon

Paris

April 11, 1953

Dear Ronnie,

I'm glad one of us is growing up. It sometimes seems to me I've just grown old, without managing any maturity at all. I may have known more when I was young. Back before you were even born, I actually wrote a novel. It made a little splash at the time, and then it went away. It was part fiction, part memoir, about a man I knew, a strange, friendless man named Gatsby, one of nature's knaves and noblemen. He was my neighbor one summer on Long Island, and then he was murdered. He made such an impression on me that I wrote a story about him, and about some other people I knew.

Then I decided I was too grown up for such silliness, and it was time that I entered the real world. That was when I went into advertising, and married Margery, and we had Alden, and I decided I owed it to him to be a good, responsible father. Which meant working late every night, rarely seeing him, ultimately sending him away to boarding school in the East--the Millbrook School for Boys, where he wrote me about being bullied by an older boy named Bill Buckley. He retaliated by telling everyone he was going to vote for Henry Wallace when he grew up, and in short order he was expelled from the school.

Would I have been a better father to Alden if I'd remained a starving novelist? I don't know. But now, I find myself looking back and wondering if I really wasted all those years, wondering if I had more books inside me waiting to come out. If I still have. Well, life has many mysteries.

You, Ronnie, are one of the sweeter of those mysteries. In your last few letters I've felt the change in you, and I realize that my old image of you as a naïve and innocent child no longer applies. Innocent, yes, and perhaps still trailing a few wisps of the naiveté I remember, but I can see that you're a woman now. Unfortunately for me, you are a very young woman, and I am fast on my way to becoming a very old man. Because you are the one person to whom I find my thoughts turning these days when life has me spinning like a dervish and staggering like a Bowery rum-pot. I hope you will take no offense when I say that if I were a younger man, Ronnie, and a better man, I would certainly find myself thinking of you in a way that my age and imperfections rule out of the question.

Your Friend,
Nick

4/12/53

FROM: MLLE CHRISTINE JORGENSEN
HOTEL D'ANGLETERRE
COPENHAGEN

TO: JAKE BARNES
PARIS HERALD TRIBUNE

JAKE DEAREST CALL ME STOP HOT PILLOW TALK
STOP LOVE CHRISTINE

Hotel de l'Odeon

Paris

April 12, 1953
By messenger to the Paris Herald Tribune

Jake--

Well, hallelujah and glory be! I've done it. I've written that novel.

Well, okay, I haven't. But I've set pen to paper with serious intent.

It feels good. It feels terrible. It feels strange as bloody hell. I feel like a virgin - "It hurts! Don't stop!" And it's all your fault, you sonofabitch. I date this fall from grace to the day you introduced me to Sartre and De Beauvoir as "Carraway, the American author." Now don't tell me I got it wrong, and what you really said was "Carraway, the other American."

Doctor, I've got this disease. I carry a notebook around with me all the time and scribble the most ridiculous goddamn shit. I scrawl notes on menus and metro tickets. Cryptic notes to myself that seem profound as hell when I write them, and later on when I excavate them from my pocket and read them they look like the ravings of a hophead.

There's an idea. I'll become a reefer addict. I'm halfway there anyway--I've started smoking those things Sartre smokes. I think they've made me shorter.

Jesus, Jake, I don't know another soul in the world I could talk to about this. Certainly not Sartre, who intimidates the crap out of me as he pats my hand and stares at me through those coke bottles he wears. "We writers," he says, "we have a responsibility to write." Like what he does and what I'm trying to do could be described by the same word. I've sat across a table from Ike, and believe me, Sartre is a lot more intimidating.

So far it's all just scraps and fragments. Have sketched out a few plot lines, a few novel ideas, but not sure any of them are going anywhere. Here's a story I've been thinking about: a guy, maybe a war vet, living in the suburbs in the house with the wife and the kids and the dog. He's doing okay doing something he likes, but he wants more. You know, more stuff, bigger house, bigger car, bigger dog. So he takes an executive job in a corporation, puts on a gray flannel suit, and starts negotiating the corporate ladder. Compromises, sells out, drinks too much, learns valuable lessons about self and society. Whaddya think? I know, I can hear you saying it.

Crap.

Which is why I'm doing this by letter. If I tried out something like that to your face I'd get about as far as "a guy."

Wilson's back in town--Sloan Wilson, you remember him? Nice young writer chap from Connecticut or Casablanca or one of those exotic places that starts with a 'C.' He was with that young crowd at Jimmy Jones's flat that night you got so tight you passed out in the pissoir. Come to think of it, you probably don't remember him. He's been in Germany, heading back to Connecticut or Casablanca. I'll run the idea past him over steak frites at Balzar tonite. If he likes it, I'll know it's shit.

God will sort it all out when He wakes up. In the meantime, let's get together soon. The booze doesn't taste right without you.

Your Devoted Friend,

Nick (of the Gillette Nicks)

Jake Barnes

April 12, 1953

by messenger

Nick my lad,

About fucking time, is all I can say. Stay with it. Scraps and fragments are where it all starts. Don't throw any of them out, at least not yet. You never know where that one true sentence that starts it all off is going to come from, and sometimes you don't recognize when you write it ... days or weeks or months later, you'll open up an old notebook, and then it's Geez, I wrote that? Don't even remember ... I must be a fucking genius.

But I don't think the chap in the gray flannel suit is the way to go. It feels like something you already wrote and rejected--almost like Trimalchio in West Egg without the Gatsby character. Like resurrecting the other guy twenty years later, and who'd want to read that?

And what else would you put into it? You'd be writing out of memory, and out of anger.

You need a love-hate relationship with your characters. You've got to take pure sadistic delight in watching them get hit by baseballs and trains and flying gash, but you've got to love 'em at the same time. I don't see you loving this fellow.

Get a little farther outside yourself. Find a character you know, but don't understand. And stay with it. Let's pass up the Deux Magots this evening. Keep your ass in the chair and write.

Conscience regards,

Ye Olde Jake

April 13, 1953

Brett darling,

I'm making my preparations to leave the ashram tomorrow. Darrell contacted me, from Teheran. He's sending someone here to brief me on what he wants me to do.

Darrell is such a strange man. I feel as though I can trust him completely, and then I'm not sure. It was he who made me see the vanity and superficiality of wanting to change the world. He made me realize that the world is within my own soul. Those of us who have achieved some measure of inner knowledge have a responsibility to use it to guide the destinies of the less enlightened.

At least I think that's right. Sometimes my mind feels so clouded I don't know what to believe any more. The only thing I'm sure of is the truth I found in your arms. You never had that kind of relationship with Darrell, did you? But no, of course you didn't. You're a little older than me, and you've had more experience in some ways, but I know I couldn't feel the way I do about you if you weren't pure in your heart.

Anyway, Darrell is sending this guy to see me, and he'll be here tonight. Actually, you know him — Lamont Cranston. I remember you telling me about Cranston and the secret wisdom he learned in the Orient. I hope he'll be able to help me unclouds my mind. Darrell says Cranston has an important assignment for me. I'm glad. I'm ready to take on something meaningful.

Love,

Olsen

(ENCRYPTED AND DECODED)
(4/13)
FROM: NICHOLAS CARRAWAY
TO: ALLEN DULLES

THANKS FOR CONCERN AND REASSURANCE. LIFE IN TATTERS, FRIENDS GONE, MARRIAGE OVER. WELL, ILL WIND THAT BLOWS NO GOOD. WHAT DO YOU MEAN, BRING BARNES IN? THOUGHT I WAS OUT OF THIS. BARNES IS A FRIEND. HAD NOT BEEN DEVELOPING HIM AS SOURCE, OR AGENT. WHY DIDN'T YOU TELL ME SOONER? NOT SURE IT CAN BE DONE NOW.

CARRAWAY

(ENCRYPTED AND DECODED) (4/13)
FROM: ALLEN DULLES
TO: NICHOLAS CARRAWAY

TELLING YOU NOW. STOP WHINING. BRING BARNES IN. PLAN UNCHANGED. COORDINATE NEWSPAPERS, STREET DEMONSTRATIONS, MILITARY UNREST, GOVERNMENT INSECURITY IN PARIS. START PLANTING STORIES.

DULLES

Paris
April 14, 1953

Dear Chris,

So, now that you're a woman, you can't keep a secret?

I heard from your Dr. Hamburger. For once in my life I don't know what the hell to say. You know, I told you that night that you were my first man, and you told me that it didn't really count, because you weren't really a man. At first I put it down to fag talk, but it turned out that you were just telling it straight.

I wasn't. There was one other time.

It was not long after the war. The first war. Those years I didn't know what the hell I was. Half man, half mad. I went after gash like a fury. God knows why. I kept taking girls to bed. And they'd laugh. Or get angry. Or worst of all, be sensitive and understanding.

I'd been playing tennis with this guy named Robert. He wasn't one of us. That made it easier. He was built like a tough guy--he'd been a boxer in college. Middleweight champion of Princeton. That didn't mean much to me, but it meant a lot to Robert. Pretty, looked a bit like Mel Ferrer. He told me it was his first time, too, but he seemed to know what he was doing. Then hated himself when the lights were on.

It was just that one time. Hell, that was enough to tell me it wasn't what I wanted, though it felt good while it was happening. Christ, anything feels good while it's happening.

Robert wouldn't leave me alone after that. Started hanging around with my friends. Strutted and flexed his muscles a lot. Invited himself along on trips. Made a play for Brett. She went to bed with him a couple of times. She told me. She always tells me. She dropped him for the bullfighter and he made a total ass of himself, and then we didn't see him anymore.

And after that, nothing. Hell, nobody was fucking anyway, in the Thirties. Everyone getting married, or getting into politics, or worrying about war. Brett would come up sometimes and crawl in bed with me. Mostly, she just wanted to be held. That's something women think is swell, being held. Let me know if it starts appealing to you, and then I'll know you've really made the switch.

It was a damn good time to be a journalist in Europe, You could still talk to the crazies around Hitler, as long as you weren't a kike--Christ, I am living in the past, aren't I? After I spent a little time with Goebbels and Speer and those bastards, I stopped using words like that.

The War was something else. Everything was raw, everything on the edge. Murrow told me that when he was broadcasting up on those rooftops--"This is London"--and the bombs were crashing around him, there were women literally crawling after him out on the roofs.

But no more sex for me. Until that night I met you. What did we do? Whatever it was, it seemed to work. And whatever it was, I guess we couldn't do it again the same way, could we? And what are we to each other, now? Friends? That doesn't seem to cover it. All I know is, since that night, Brett doesn't break my heart any more.

Fuck it. I can't live like this, and you get the blame. Or the credit. I'm going to Copenhagen.

Love,

Jake

4/14/53

FROM: LADY BRETT ASHLEY
GRAND HOTEL
NEW DELHI

TO: LARRY DARRELL
TEHERAN

DONT WORRY ABOUT KID STOP HES RIPE STOP ONE SESSION WITH CRANSTON AND HES YOURS STOP JUST ONE THING DARLING DONT EVER ASK ME TO GO TO BED WITH CRANSTON AGAIN STOP HES TOO KINKY EVEN FOR ME

BRETT

4/14/53

TO: REZA PAHLAVI
TEHERAN

REZA HONEY STOP SIT TIGHT STOP BY THIS TIME NEXT WEEK WILL BE SITTING IN YOUR LAP ON PEACOCK THRONE

LOVE BRETT

Apartment C
14½ MacDougal Street
New York

April 14, 1953

Dear Nick,

First of all, let me start out by saying that I never thought of you as old. I've always thought of you as my rock, though, from way back when Snicklepoo and the Baby Sitter was just starting--and wow, does that ever seem like a long time ago!--a whole lifetime or two. When things were going wrong on the set--anything from cameras breaking down to worries about the schedule to was I wearing the right color dress, I always knew, and everyone always knew, that you'd solve the problem. But did you know that whenever you passed through the set, all the girls--the makeup girl, the head writer, everyone--would turn their heads around just to watch you, and they'd giggle and whisper, "He's so sexy."

And you know, I was so naïve back then, I'm not sure I even knew what sexy was, exactly, except maybe Eddie Fisher. So, you see, my first definition of sexy was you! I guess you think that's pretty silly, coming from a mere girl. But it's true.

And you're not old.

Yours always,

Ronnie

Margery Pyle
40125 Oak Park Drive
Oak Park, Illinois

April 14, 1953

Nicholas,

I am back from Reno, and the divorce is final. In the absence of any compelling argument from your lawyer, the judge granted all my property settlement and alimony requests.

I am making a new life for myself. I've met a fine man. His name is William Fromme, he's an executive with Welch's Grape Juice, and he's been working with Mr. Welch to start a new anti-Communist society that will continue Senator McCarthy's fine work. He has a little daughter, Lynette, and he's raising her to be a real patriotic American. We won't make the same mistakes with her that we did--that you did--with our son.

Anyway, I just want to tell you that if I ever had any questions about your manhood--and I did--and I know you did --I just want to reassure you. You don't measure up to a real man.

Margery

Apartment C
14½ MacDougal Street
New York

April 14, 1953

Dear Nick,

I found Trimalchio in West Egg at the Strand Bookstore, and I read it through in one sitting, and I loved it! It's everything that I ~~love~~ like so much about you--beautiful language, wise insights, and such wonderful sympathy for how people can make mistakes, and it only makes them more human. I can just feel the love you have for all your characters, even the awful ones, like Tom. I wonder--was Jordan based on Mrs. Carraway at all?

You're a wonderful writer! I just wish you had written more novels. Well, it's not too late. I believe there can be second acts in all of our lives.

Ruth--Ruth Brown, her full name is--took me to a recording session yesterday. I was secretly hoping she'd ask me to sing backup on it, but then I got there, and I listened to the musicians Jerry had there, and the backup singers, and I was praying they wouldn't. Needless to say, they didn't.

She recorded four songs. I loved them all, but the one I liked best was called "Mama, He Treats Your Daughter Mean." Now, I can sing about mamas and daughters, but not like that. When Ruth sang it, you just knew she wasn't really calling her Mama for help. It's like, when she sings "Mama!" she's just telling the world she's got problems with a no-good man, but she's proud that she's woman enough to handle them. I wonder if I'll ever be woman enough to sing a song like that.

After the session, she took me up to a night club in Harlem called Smalls Paradise. There was a jazz quartet playing there, and they asked Ruth to get up and sing a number with them. She sang "Willow, Weep For Me," and it took my breath away. It's so different from the way she sings at the recording session. It seemed ... oh, here's where I realize I don't know anything about music, and I have so much to learn, but it seemed to me like it was different with the musicians. In the recording studio, singing the blues, she seemed to be listening to the rhythm section, and singing with them, but at Smalls Paradise she seemed to be listening to all the instruments, and almost becoming one of them.

I've never felt music like I felt it last night. I don't know if I could ever learn to do it, not the way Ruthie does. But there's something about New York that makes you feel like you can reinvent yourself, and everything is possible. I wish you were here.

Wishing,

Ronnie

PS. Jerry has given me records by Billie Holiday, Ella Fitzgerald, Dinah Washington, Chris Connor, and Anita O'Day, and I'm spending the day listening to them.

(ENCRYPTED AND DECODED)
(4/15)
FROM: IRVING KRISTOL
TO: LARRY DARRELL

HERE'S THE LATEST BATCH OF HEADLINE STORIES, NEWS FEATURE ITEMS, AND EDITORIALS FOR THE TEHERAN PRESS. WE'LL NEED A CHECKLIST ON OUR PLANS. REMEMBER, THIS CAN'T GO WRONG. WE'LL ONLY GET ONE CHANCE AT THAT CRYING COMMIE.

KRISTOL

(ENCRYPTED AND DECODED)
(4/15)
FROM: LARRY DARRELL
TO: IRVING KRISTOL

STORIES DISPATCHED TO THE LOCAL PRESS. MILITARY SALTED WITH OUR MEN, READY FOR THE COUP. GANG OF THUGS ROAMING THE STREETS BREAKING WINDOWS, SHOUTING "DOWN WITH MOSSADEGH!" NOW WE'VE UNLEASHED A SECOND GANG OF BIGGER, UGLIER THUGS TO BEAT UP THE FIRST GANG AND SHOUT "MOSSADEGH FOREVER! COMMUNISM FOR IRAN!" SYMPATHY FOR THE ANTI-M THUGS, CHAOS AND PANIC IN THE STREETS.

DARRELL

(ENCRYPTED AND DECODED)
(4/15)
FROM: IRVING KRISTOL
TO: LARRY DARRELL

IT HAD BETTER BE ENOUGH.
KRISTOL

(ENCRYPTED AND DECODED)
(4/15)
FROM: LARRY DARRELL
TO: IRVING KRISTOL

IRVING, YOU'RE TURNING INTO AN OLD WOMAN.

DARRELL

Hotel de l'Odeon

Paris

April 15, 1953
By messenger to the Paris Herald Tribune

Jake--

Notes, ideas, pieces. I don't remember Trimalchio being this hard to lift off the ground. It was hard to sustain, Lord knows, although even then, huge chunks of it seemed to write themselves, until I went back and looked at them, and discovered that they needed a whole lot more help from me before they were ready to go out into the world. But I never had any doubts about what I wanted to write, or where it was heading. Maybe it had to do with being young and foolish. But mostly, I suspect, it was because I really didn't know I was going to be writing a novel. I just knew I had this story that I had to lay out in front of me. Now it's just the reverse. I know I want to write something. I want to find characters and let them loose on a story. I want to hold a mirror up to the world. I want to make a difference. I want to explore corners of the human psyche, and I want to unleash the power of words to illuminate the darkness and find paths around corners and discover uncharted islands where the natives practice customs no one has ever heard of before. I want words that will seduce women and turn grown men into boys again. I know that it matters.

And I don't have a story.

Ideas, by all means. Will-'o-the wisp ideas, prickles of current waiting to turn of a sudden to St. Elmo's fire and turn my typewriter into a blaze of light. And you're right, I don't want to turn a microscope on the flea circus of advertising. They can make you itch, but magnified to the hundredth degree, they're still just performing fleas.

So I'm looking for a character. I've been thinking about Alden ... he's the one I perhaps need most to understand. I wonder if I could write a novel from the point of view of a young man like him ... of a boy in the process of becoming a young man. I was thinking of the year that we sent Alden to an eastern prep school, which he left abruptly before the end of the semester, went into New York and wandered around, haunted by the sense that the world was full of phonies.

There's a character ... maybe not a character I know well enough. And is it enough of a story?
Or do I need a story at all? What if I

create the Nick that never was? Did you know that after Jimmy Gatz died, and I went home and moved back in with my parents and did all that soul-searching that wound up being Trimalchio, I almost said the hell with it all? I was on the brink of just dropping everything and hobo-ing it around the country. I wonder if I could recreate that alter ego. Maybe make him younger, change the time frame ... a World War II vet, chasing along on the road from one end of the country to the other.

What do you think? Do I have anything yet? Anything worth pursuing? I keep thinking I'll know it when I hit it, but what if I don't?

Spinning like a top,

Nick

Kempinksi Hotel
Berlin

April 16, 1953

Jake dear,

You silly old bear. If you can't say it, I can.

I love you.

Even if it's the love that wouldn't even begin to know how to speak its name.

Thank you for telling me more about yourself. I treasure it, I really do. I want to know all about you.

I'll be traveling for a couple of speaking engagements, but I'll get back to see you as soon as I can. Dr. Hamburger is a dear. A big, brawny, outdoorsy Scandinavian type--you'd like him. And a sports fan. He says his ambition is to be the Stein Ericksen of sex surgery. A little jealous, dear? No need. He's too young for me. You know I prefer old grizzly bears like you.

I don't understand war, and I suppose I never will. When I was thirteen and the war was just starting, I jumped up and down a lot and yelled about wanting to go over and kill Japs, but inside I knew I didn't really mean it.

I've always been drawn to the intensity of experience, and I've always held back from it. Sex ... well, how could I open myself up completely when I didn't know who I was? I didn't want to make love to women, and I didn't want to make love to the kind of man who wanted to make love to a man.

I was too late for the war. I was drafted right after the armistice. I was relieved, and I was disappointed. I don't think I'm a physical coward, though I was always a sissy. I never minded being beaten up as a kid, as much as I minded that they wanted to do it. I wouldn't have been afraid of being hurt, or even of dying, as much as the possibility that I'd have to kill someone. I know you were a medical corpsman in the first war, and a journalist in the second, so you weren't directly involved in the business of killing people, except to the extent that everyone in a war is in that business. And you always knew that you might have to kill someone.

There was a sergeant in my basic training at Fort Dix. He'd been at Anzio, won the Silver Star with clusters. He was the toughest guy I'd ever met, and probably the bravest. And he had his secrets, and his torments. Including the one you're maybe thinking, but that was almost the least of it.

I sucked his cock, but what he really wanted was to suck mine. I tried to tell him I didn't do that, I didn't care about my cock, but I could see that it meant so much to him. But what he really needed came later, when I held him in my arms like a little boy, and he told me about the men--boys, really--he had killed. Described their faces to me. Every one of them. This tough, tough sergeant. I'd never heard him talk in anything except four-letter words. But he was almost poetic when he was describing their faces. And he remembered every one.

Men have it so hard. With all the heartache, I'm glad I am what I am.

Love, Christine

SPECIAL TO THE

New York Herald Tribune

APRIL 16, 1953

MOSSADEGH VICTORY ANNOUNCED

TEHERAN -- The Ministry of the Interior announced tonight that the Government had won the plebiscite on Premier Mohammed Mossadegh's appeal for authority to dissolve the Majlis (Parliament) by 2,043,389 votes to 1,207. The official announcement cleared the way for the President to dissolve the chamber, which he may do in a nationwide broadcast tomorrow.

(ENCRYPTED AND DECODED)
(4/16)
FROM: IRVING KRISTOL
TO: LARRY DARRELL

WHAT THE HELL? WE WERE SUPPOSED TO RIG THE MAJLIS TO THROW MOSSADEGH OUT! WHAT'S GOING WRONG?
KRISTOL

(ENCRYPTED AND DECODED)
(4/16)
FROM: LARRY DARRELL
TO: IRVING KRISTOL

DON'T WORRY. WE HAVE THE MILITARY.

DARRELL

Jake Barnes

By Messenger
April 16, 1953

Dear Nick--

What the hell, Nick, what the hell.

Writing doesn't have to be like that. Jesus, we'd all shoot ourselves. You're a good man, but you work too hard. Just remember what I keep telling you--find that one true sentence, write it down, and the rest followeth like a pack of mangy dogs after a bitch in heat.

As for seducing grown women and turning boys into men, these are adventures that can exist outside the written page. It can all be fuckingly complicated, but maybe worth the while.

Meanwhile, here's your chance to get your feet wet again. After I finish tomorrow's column, I'm heading up to Denmark for a couple of weeks. I'm going to ask you to fill in for me for one of those weeks. I've got that kid Buchwald from the copy desk set for the other. I'll fill you in when I can.

Yours,
Jake

PS. Thanks for minding the store.

New York Herald Tribune
PARIS EDITION, APRIL 17, 1953

THE BARNES DOOR

PARIS--When I was ten years old, my old man took me to the Tercentenary Exposition in Jamestown, Virginia. I ate Jell-O, and I saw moving pictures, and I watched a carriage move along a street without a horse attached to it. My father told me "Son, America is the greatest country in the world." I believed it then, and I believe it now.

The difference is that then I thought it was an eternal truth, as infinite as the air we breathe. Now I know it's something we have to work at to keep it that way. Work hard. Every day of our lives.

You see, it doesn't take much to let a beautiful dream go sour. All it takes is a few bad people getting busy, and a few good people getting lazy. At the end of the war I saw an America that was looked to as a beacon of hope and a bastion of liberty throughout the world, if not always by the governments, then certainly by the people. I'm talking about the guys who worked in the fields and the factories and the offices, who prayed in churches and synagogues, who dreamed of one day being able to raise their families in freedom, and who believed that America would be their champion. That's the way America looked to them then, and I thought that would last my lifetime.

Now I'm getting uneasy. I'm not saying it's gone, not by a long shot. But Americans who fought for freedom are being told today that freedom has its limits. There's a frenzy loose in Washington, where a man I know was hounded out of his job and robbed of his good name with nobody bothering to give a reason. "They don't need reasons," he told me. "Reason just slows them down. It's more like the fascism we fought than the principles we fought it with." The thugs in Washington are riding roughshod over the rights that looked so inalienable just a few short years ago, and if the real Americans don't speak up, those rights won't be there when we go to look for them.

I hear the people who run things may not be content to trample American constitutional rights. There's a certain popular government in the Middle East, a government of the people, by the people, and for the people, that is in very real danger of perishing from this earth. It could happen because there are shadowy, cold-faced men in the air-conditioned halls of Washington who think it suits their purposes, and don't believe there's anything that can stop them.

And it's starting to happen right now. There are forces at work in that certain country right now, buying the cooperation of newspapers, fermenting military unrest, coordinating street demonstrations -- hiring thugs to break windows and rough up storekeepers while carrying signs denouncing the government, then hiring more thugs to do the same while carrying signs praising the government.

When we start protecting America by denying freedom at home and imposing our will abroad, it may not matter anymore how many movies and automobiles we have, or even how much Jell-O. If we want to go on being the greatest country in the world, we need to think hard about what made us that in the first place.

Note: Jake Barnes will be on vacation for the next two weeks. In this space, enjoy columns by Art Buchwald next week, and Nicholas Carraway the following week.

(ENCRYPTED AND DECODED)
(4/17)
FROM: NICHOLAS CARRAWAY
TO: ALLEN DULLES

BARNES LEAK NOT FROM ME. BARNES MUST HAVE HAD COLUMN IN BEFORE I HEARD FROM YOU. I REMAIN A PATRIOT, WOULD NEVER REVEAL CONFIDENTIAL INFORMATION. TELL ME WHAT I CAN DO TO HELP TURN THIS SITUATION AROUND.

CARRAWAY

(ENCRYPTED AND DECODED)
(4/17)
FROM: LARRY DARRELL
TO: ALLEN DULLES

GOT AN OPERATIVE I NEED YOU TO INSTALL IN EMBASSY IN TEHRAN. MAKE HIM CHARGÉ D'AFFAIRES OR WHATEVER THE HELL YOU WANT TO CALL HIM TO GIVE HIM STANDING. NAME: ALDEN CARRAWAY. FILE BEING DELIVERED BY HAND. CRUCIAL.

DARRELL

SPECIAL TO THE
New York Herald Tribune
APRIL 17, 1953

MOSSADEGH CHARGES DISTORTION ON IRAN

TEHERAN--PremierMohammed Mossadegh broadcast his thanks today to the Iranian people for their plebiscite vote dissolving the Majlis, then accused "some world statesmen" of misinterpreting and distorting events in Iran.

"Some foreigners endeavor to misinterpret and distort any step the Iranian nation takes to realize its aspirations because the Iranian people have forged a bond of unity and are resolved to cut off the hands that foreigners have extended into their country, which is the very thing of which a particular group is afraid."

(ENCRYPTED AND DECODED)
(4/18)
FROM: IRVING KRISTOL
TO: LARRY DARRELL

WHOSE HANDS IS HE TALKING ABOUT? STRONGLY SUGGEST ABORTING MISSION.
KRISTOL

(ENCRYPTED AND DECODED)
(4/18)
FROM: LARRY DARRELL
TO: IRVING KRISTOL

DON'T WORRY. HE DOESN'T MEAN US. MOSSY FIGURES IT'S THE BRITISH. HE WON'T KNOW WHAT HIT HIM.

DARRELL

Hotel D'Angleterre
KONGENS NYTORV 34
COPENHAGEN, DENMARK

April 19

Dear Chris,

Trip was swell. Sat across the aisle from a young Danish wench who kept looking at me with contemplative gravity. Like she was sizing up a bull at auction. Displayed my return ticket prominently in my lap. As if to say catch me on the way back, honey, when I'm better prepared. Did I mention she was a nun?

Your Dr. Hamburger met me at the station. Eager sonofabitch, ain't he? Thought he was going to perform the surgery in the goddam cab. Positively effervescent after examination--I'm a textbook candidate--of course, it's his fucking textbook--he's having the operating theater enlarged and inviting camera crews from Pathé News--and Louella Parsons and Dorothy Kilgallen will be on hand to broadcast the operation live over Mutual Radio. All contingent naturally on my okay.

Ah, there's the $64 question. Do I speak now, or forever hold my piece? I feel like you're the only person in the world who might understand my dilemma, and then I reflect that you went the other way and have no idea what the fuck I'm talking about. Don't mind me, Chris--we writing chaps have words by the thousands--dozens, anyway--to choose from, and I have but to make my choice from two:

Yes or No?

Or there's Maybe ...

Love always,

Jake

Hotel de l'Odeon

Paris

April 19, 1953

Dear Ronnie,

I asked Jake if he had ever heard of Ruth Brown, and he hadn't, but he knows this little tiny shop where they have the latest American records, and he went and bought some of hers.

Then he went back to the shop a few hours later and bought every record on your friend Jerry's label.

I think Jake is really starting to miss the USA. I'm not so sure I am. Except for one person.

With much affection,

Nick

SPECIAL TO THE

New York Herald Tribune

APRIL 19, 1953

SHAH FLEES IRAN AFTER MOVE TO DISMISS MOSSADEGH FAILS

TEHERAN -- Shah Mohammed Reza Pahlevi and his Queen fled to Baghdad, Iraq, today after a coup attempt to oust Premier Mohammed Mossadegh had failed. Dr. Mossadegh appeared to be in complete control tonight, with the bulk of the Army apparently supporting him.

The attempt to remove the Premier was made at midnight. By dawn, Government forces had freed arrested officials, and had in their turn arrested Colonel Nasiri, commander of the palace guard, and scores of other persons, including military officers. The stroke and counterstroke were carried out without bloodshed.

The 72-year-old Premier clearly was master of the situation, at least for the time being, but the details of just what happened are confused.

(ENCRYPTED AND DECODED)

(4/19)

FROM: IRVING KRISTOL

TO: LARRY DARRELL

MISSION HAS FAILED. IMPERATIVE YOU GET OUT OF IRAN AT ONCE.

KRISTOL

Hotel de l'Odeon

Paris

April 19, 1953

Dear Ronnie,

I received a cryptic note from Jake, who has hied himself off to Denmark for reasons unstated. So I'm alone with a bottle of aquavit and my thoughts.

I'm glad you liked Trimalchio in West Egg. I feel so damned distant from it now, and yet in a way it feels like the only decent thing I've ever done with my life.

After Jimmy Gatz died, when I sat down to write about him, I didn't know I was going to write a novel, or even what writing a novel meant. Hell, I didn't even know I was going to write. I just knew that before I could get on with my life, I had to figure out what had just happened.

The notes that became Trimalchio were the beginnings of me trying to figure out not just who Gatz was, but why he was so damned important to me. The more I wrote, the more the writing itself started to matter. I found that I didn't simply want to understand what was important; I wanted to find the words to express it.

As the days slipped into weeks, and the weeks into months--well, a few months--the emphasis started to shift. I was still trying to figure out Gatz, but I found myself more and more loving the process of writing. I was going back over the stuff I'd written, not just to make sure I'd gotten it right, but to make sure I'd written it well ... and I didn't really even know what good writing was. I just knew that I was starting to hear words differently, and that suddenly I cared more than I could say about how words sounded, and how they looked when they started grouping together on a page.

I finished the writing, and I sent it to a publisher, and wonder of wonders, it came out as a book. It's like babies, or spinning gold from straw, I have no idea how it works. The book got a few good reviews, and a few bad ones, and was otherwise massively ignored by the incognoscenti. I suspect that the title didn't help. No one knew what the hell

"Trimalchio" meant. It's a literary allusion, which is the kiss of death--the original Trimalchio was a character in Petronius's The Satyricon, a coarse parvenu who is respected by no one, and whose only entrée into polite society is his money. (Over here in France, observing Americans throwing their weight and money around, I wonder if our country may be the Gatsby, the Trimalchio, of the postwar era.)

So the book sank beneath the swells of public notice, and after Margery and I got engaged, it was understood that my little writing aberration was at an end. In years to come, my mother would refer to it as "that time when you had the flu."

Now ... it's probably too late. It's probably too late for a lot of things, and maybe I never had the equipment to start with. And I still don't know what good writing is. It's not too late for you, though. I remember when we hired you for Snicklepoo and the Baby Sitter. You were what ... nineteen? We were looking for someone who could relate to children, but could also project on television. To me, that meant someone who could sing a song. To our director, Jimmie Dodd, it meant,

"It doesn't matter how old they are. The only thing that sells on television is sex. What I'd really like is to find a girl who's just starting to develop, and let the audience tune in to see how much her titties have grown every week."

Oh, lord. I shouldn't have said that. But I'm trying not to edit myself with you anymore. Something's been growing in this correspondence, something every bit as mysterious and wonderful as the process Jimmie Dodd referred to, and I think we need to see each other one of these fine days to figure out just what it is. Your side of the Atlantic, or mine?

I listened to the singers you mentioned in your letter. Jake had a few of them, and I bought the rest from that little record store I told you about. I'd really never heard any of them, except Ella Fitzgerald. I liked all of them--especially Chris Connor. That smoky voice of hers reminds me of the youth I wish I'd had. It sounds like the way the Jazz Age should have been.

Love,

Nick

PS. Jake left his Trib column in my custody while he's on his Denmark retreat. I'm to split the duties with a young fellow named Buchwald. I'm making him go first. What the hell am I going to write about?

SPECIAL TO THE
New York Herald Tribune
APRIL 19, 1953

SHAH TO GO ON TO PARIS

BAGHDAD -- Shah Mohammed Reza Pahlavi arrived here unexpectedly in his private plane after Iran's Premier Mossadegh had crushed an attempted military coup by officers of the Shah's Imperial Guard. With the Shah were his queen, Soraya, an aide and a pilot.

Neither had any luggage; piles of clothes belonging to the royal couple were strewn inside the twin-engined Beechcraft plane.

The Shah, 33, and his wife, 21, planned to travel from Baghdad to Paris. After high-level government consultations, they were escorted to the government's guest house.

The Shah's aide emphasized that he has not abdicated and did not intend to abdicate.

Meanwhile in Teheran, pro-Mossadegh mobs threw down from their pedestals statues of Shah Mohammed Reza. As crowds began battering the statue in Parliament Square, the Communists were driven off by police, but Nationalist, Paniranist, and Socialist bands were allowed to continue the destruction unmolested.

For two hours, men sawed at the ankles of the bronze statue, while others chanted songs written overnight on the flight of the Shah. Finally, a motorized crane was brought into action and the statue was toppled with a great clank amid loud cheers.

Similar anti-Shah sentiment was shown by the removal of virtually all his pictures from homes, restaurants, offices, and even Government Ministries.

(ENCRYPTED AND DECODED)
(4/20)
FROM: ALLEN DULLES
TO: LARRY DARRELL

OUR REPORTS SAY MOBS IN STREET HEAVILY PRO-MOSSADEGH. YOU'VE BOTCHED IT.

DULLES

(ENCRYPTED AND DECODED)
(4/20)
FROM: LARRY DARRELL
TO: ALLEN DULLES

DOESN'T MATTER, AS LONG AS THEY'RE IN THE STREETS. SITUATION JUST WHERE I WANT IT.

DARRELL

(ENCRYPTED AND DECODED)
(4/20)
FROM: ALLEN DULLES
TO: LARRY DARRELL

MISSION IS ABORTED. REPEAT, ABORTED. GET OUT OF TEHERAN AT ONCE. TOO DANGEROUS. WE ARE NO LONGER IN THE COUP BUSINESS.

DULLES

(ENCRYPTED AND DECODED)
(4/20)
FROM: LARRY DARRELL
TO: ALLEN DULLES

ARE YOU KIDDING? I'VE JUST BEGUN TO FIGHT! CARRAWAY CARD READY TO PLAY. DO YOU REALIZE WE HAVE A CHANCE TO OVERTHROW A REAL GOVERNMENT? THIS IS BETTER THAN TANTRIC SEX!

DARRELL

(ENCRYPTED AND DECODED)
(4/21)
FROM: ALLEN DULLES
TO: LARRY DARRELL

WHERE ARE YOU? REPORT IN AT ONCE. I REPEAT--WE ARE NO LONGER IN THE COUP BUSINESS. SHAH PLANNING TO ANNOUNCE ABDICATION AFTER WE DEBRIEF HIM. WE NEED TO HEAR FROM YOU RIGHT AWAY.

DULLES

(ENCRYPTED AND DECODED)
(4/21)
FROM: P. RADCLIFFE JONES
TO: ALLEN DULLES

UNABLE TO LOCATE MR. DARRELL TO DELIVER YOUR LAST CABLE. WHEREABOUTS UNKNOWN.

P. RADCLIFFE JONES, DEPUTY COUNSELOR OF

EMBASSY

Hotel de l'Odeon

Paris

April 22, 1953

Dear Jake,

Have fun in Copenhagen. What the hell are you doing in Copenhagen?

I flipped a coin with Buchwald. He lost, so he goes first on babysitting your column. He tells me he plans to do an exposé of the New York Yankees. He claims they have a deal with the Devil, and he has the papers to prove it. I intend to follow up with a column on the scandal of escargot farming in the Parisian sewers. Little girls on leashes forced to sniff them out, fed only on martinis. The little girls, not the escargots. Or maybe both. I'm still investigating.

Yours in journalistic solidarity and abject terror,

Nick

PS. Tell me something. You're a man of the world, or so I've heard--mostly from you, as I recall. I probably couldn't have asked you this in person, but I'm sitting here in this ridiculous French bathtub with my knees tucked up under my chin holding the sorry remains of a bottle of aquavit, and I'm thinking about something Margery said to me more than once. She said I could never make a woman happy because of the way I was built. You know, the old tool of manhood department. How about it, Jake? Is size really the measure of a man?

Give my regards to Hans Christian Andersen.

Teheran, April 23

Alden--

Can't meet you in person. I'm laying low. I've arranged for you to meet with Dr. Mossadegh. Your diplomatic standing is all set. Tell Mossy that as a representative of the American people you're concerned about American families who are being harassed. Tell him that innocent children are answering the family phone and being subjected to unspeakable threats and vile language. Tell him that you're appealing to his sense of decency and fair play to do something about it. Be yourself, kid. You have that American openness that he likes.

Larry

Hotel D'Angleterre
KONGENS NYTORV 34
COPENHAGEN, DENMARK

April 23, 1953

Dear Christine,

Get a load of the enclosed PS from Nick. Is he trying to drive me CRAZY????

I've given the okay to Hamburger. The Stein Ericksen of sex surgery set to schuss tomorrow morning at 10. I'll be damned glad when this thing is over. Worst case, I guess, is no worse than it's been the last 30 years or so. Best case--what the hell is the best case, anyway?

Did you know that the Bible has a special section for people like me? It's Deuteronomy 23:1. He that is wounded in the stones, or hath his privy member cut off, shall not enter into the congregation of the Lord.

Well, that tells you something, doesn't it? The way I look at it, and I say this with the full piety of someone who's never left the Church, technically speaking, it tells me that the Kingdom of God, at least for a man, is a woman's cunt. There's probably no equivalent for women, which is maybe why women tend to me more devout than men. They have no Kingdom of God on earth to distract them.

Here's a question for you, my love. Now that you're a woman, do you think about sex less often than you did when you were a man? I'm being serious. Nick's a man, so he's got to think about it most of the time. By Christ, he talks about that damned cock of his all the time, or at least whenever he's tight. Jesus, I never saw a man so bloody insecure! But his gangster novel wasn't written with his cock. I wonder what his next book would have been like, if he'd written it. Says he's writing again now. Maybe he's ready.

As Mehitabel says, toujours gai, kid, toujours gai. All's for the best in this best of all passable worlds.

Your old Bear,

Jake

Teheran, April 23

Larry--

I'll do it. And I appreciate the confidence you've shown in me. Mossadegh is no fanatic, I'm sure he'll listen. And I'll emphasize that America has no intention of interfering in the internal affairs of a friendly country.

I won't let you down.

Alden

(ENCRYPTED AND DECODED)
(4/23)
FROM: IRVING KRISTOL
TO: KIM PHILBY

MI5 WILL NEED TO COORDINATE WITH US ON THIS, SO BE PREPARED. AFTER IRAN, THE FRENCH GOVERNMENT IS GOING DOWN, AND WE'RE GETTING OUR DUCKS IN A ROW IN INDO-CHINA. YOU SHOULD HAVE ALL CODE NAMES ON FILE. IF WE PLAN IT RIGHT, THE REDS WILL NEVER KNOW WHAT HIT THEM. THE COMMUNIST STATES WILL FALL LIKE DOMINOES, ALL THE WAY TO CHINA.

KRISTOL

American Embassy
Teheran

April 24

Dearest Brett,

I've just had the most remarkable day of my life. I met for over an hour with Dr. Mohammed Mossadegh, one on one. What an amazing man!

Dr. Mossadegh was grave but gracious. I explained to him that I was there not only as an American diplomat but as a humanitarian, and he greeted me in the name of humanitarianism everywhere. He added, however, that since I was an American diplomat, he felt it incumbent upon himself to express his displeasure at the American government's stated position of recognizing the Shah as the leader of his country, when the Shah was now nothing more than a fleeing criminal, the leader of a failed coup.
I told him that I didn't know anything about that, but that America has always stood with the poor and downtrodden of this earth.

Then I got to the heart of my mission, the harassment of American citizens in Tehran. They get threatening phone calls, often delivered to innocent children in language to which children should not be exposed.

They are harassed on the street when going about their business--even nannies pushing strollers. Their automobiles are vandalized --headlights smashed in, tires slashed, upholstery ripped out. I appealed to him as a man of decency to do something about this situation.

He didn't say anything at first. Just looked at me. There was sadness in his eyes, and something more that I couldn't identify. I just got the feeling he had seen more, and felt more, and thought about more in his lifetime than I can ever imagine.

He sat quietly for a few moments longer, and I almost thought he had forgotten I was there. And maybe he had. Suddenly he stood up without looking at me, walked to a telephone in the corner of the room, and dialed the chief of police.

His voice was heavy. "I cannot countenance what is happening to visitors to our country," he said. "Ours is a culture of courtesy. We must put an instant and complete stop to all rioting in the streets. Thank you."

Brett, Larry was right. He understood Mossadegh perfectly. The man is a responsible leader. I believe Iran is in good hands.

Love,
Alden

PS. Larry says he has another assignment for me. I'm not sure what it is, but it's in Indo-China. I can't tell you how it feels to be finally involved in a meaningful way in doing some good in the world.

PPS. For reasons of security, and for more personal reasons, I will be dropping my surname and from now on using my middle name, which is Pyle.

Kempinksi Hotel

Berlin

April 25, 1953

Dearest Jake,

Do I think less about sex? Oh, much less! I don't know how you men ever get anything done!

You know, for as long as I can remember, I've been interested in what makes someone one sex or another, and it's not always as easy as you'd think.

Have you ever heard of the slipper limpet? You've seen them, even if you haven't heard the name---they're little shellfish, and you see them in clusters at docks, like mussels, one on top of the other.

They're always one on top of the other, with the girls underneath. Mmm, I like that. The girls are also always a lot bigger, which is a lot more common in nature than you'd think. (So is losing your male equipment, for that matter--with some spiders, after the male is through servicing the female, it breaks off inside her.) The pile goes from big mamas on the bottom to little males on top. But the little guys on top are persistent. They don't call this species Crepidula fornicata for nothing. They'll extend their little wee-wees down four, five, six shells, as many as it takes, till they find a female. So you'd think the guys in the middle would be having the most fun--the lowest male and the highest female. But it doesn't work that way. You see, the big mamas on the bottom weren't always big mamas. Once, they were little males ... and as they grew bigger, they also changed sex. So the ones in the middle ... they really are in the middle. Not boys still, not girls yet.

I guess all my life, I've felt like a crepidula, mostly without the fornicata. But like that gender-jumbled fellow in the middle, and like that poor drill sergeant at Fort Dix, it means a lot to me to be held properly, by someone who'll give me strength and nurturing, erotic tenderness, and more than anything else, the sureness that it's me he's holding.

I never felt more completely like that than I did with you. And let me tell you this, you old bear, you're all man--and you always have been. You're no crepidula. And whether or not this operation succeeds (and it will--Dr. H is a genius!), you'll never have to send your wee-wee out probing around corners and under shells. Any woman who truly loves men will be coming to you, if you let them.

We'll have our time together, I know that. Maybe not a long time. I can see where your destiny is heading, even though you can't, yet. And I'm destined to be Christine Jorgensen, with all the good and bad that it will come to mean, for the rest of my life. But I'll always love you.

Good luck, darling! Break a--well, I'm not sure what. Anyway, I guess by now the deed is done! I can't wait to see you. All of you!

Love, Christine

(ENCRYPTED AND DECODED)
(4/25)
FROM: ALLEN DULLES
TO: IRVING KRISTOL

WHAT'S GOING ON IN IRAN? MOSSADEGH IS TAKING THE WEAPONS OUT OF THE HANDS OF HIS OWN FOLLOWERS.

DULLES

SPECIAL TO THE

New York Herald Tribune

APRIL 25, 1953

EXTREMIST RIOTERS IN TEHERAN FOUGHT BY POLICE AND ARMY

TEHERAN -- Policemen and soldiers, said to be acting under orders from Premier Mohammed Mossadegh, swung into action tonight against rioting Communist partisans and Nationalist extremists. The troops appeared to be in a frenzy as they smashed into the rioters with clubbed rifles and nightsticks, and hurled tear gas bombs.

According to sources inside the Mossadegh government, an unidentified representative of an American peace group had called on Premier Mossadegh earlier in the day "for the purpose of discussing recent developments in Iran." No further information was available about the meeting.

SPECIAL TO THE

New York Herald Tribune

APRIL 26, 1953

ARMY SEIZES HELM ROYALISTS IN IRAN OUST MOSSADEGH

Ex-Premier and Cabinet Flee Mobs

TEHERAN--In a swift and bloody coup, Iranians loyal to Shah Mohammed Reza Pahlavi today swept Premier Mohammed Mossadegh from power. Two hundred were estimated to have died in the fierce last-stand battle at Dr. Mossadegh's heavily fortified home.

The Army, which appeared solidly loyal to Dr. Mossadegh earlier in the week, turned on its top officers today. Dr. Mossadegh's Chief of Staff and other top officers fled long before the day was over.

The troops and the police that took part in the overthrow were led by huge mobs shouting for the return of the Shah.

4/26/53

FROM: JAKE BARNES
ROYAL HOSPITAL, COPENHAGEN

TO: MLLE CHRISTINE JORGENSEN
KEMPINSKI HOTEL,
BERLIN

ECCE HOMO

JAKE

(ENCRYPTED AND DECODED)
(4/26)
FROM: ALLEN DULLES
TO: ROBERT COHN

NO PLANS FOR COUP IN FRANCE. ELBA IS DEAD. TELL NEPHEW TO BACK OFF. REPEAT, ELBA DEAD. BACK OFF.

DULLES

(ENCRYPTED AND DECODED)
(4/26)
FROM: ROBERT COHN
TO: IRVING KRISTOL

HEY, WHAT'S WITH ALLIE? HE GETTING COLD FEET?

ROBBIE

(ENCRYPTED AND DECODED)
(4/26)
FROM: IRVING KRISTOL
TO: ROBERT COHN

COHN, YOU IDIOT, THIS IS SERIOUS. THE COUP IN IRAN VERY NEARLY BACKFIRED. WE CAN'T TAKE ANY MORE CHANCES.

KRISTOL

(ENCRYPTED AND DECODED)
(4/26)
FROM: ROBERT COHN
TO: ALLEN DULLES

ALLIE--DON'T WORRY ABOUT A THING.

ROBBIE

Hotel George V

31 Avenue George V
Paris 8eme
France

April 26

Christine baby--

I love Paris! I luv luv luv wuv wuv wuv Paris! "Daddy" says it's decadent and full of Reds, and they all hate us over here. But I've found some places where they think Americans are just the cat's pajamas. Have you ever been to a club called the Chez Miao Miao? I bet you have, you devil! And guess who took me there? None other than Maurice Chevalier!

So did you hear the news? "Daddy" made a citizen's arrest today! He's been acting all strange and sulky and I thought maybe he was mad because I've been spending so much time with Maurice, but it turns out he was hatching this really ballsy whopper of a supprise!

So you know that guy Kerraway who was at your table the other night at that stupid jazz club? You may not know it, but he was a witness in front of Sen. McCarthy's committy. Well, it turns out he really is a Red! It turns out he wrote a book a long time ago, called "Something-or-other with Egg," that the Commies have put in every library we looked at in every American embassy in Europe.

So--today "Daddy" marched right up to this cafay where Kerraway was sitting with his pal the Commie French writer Albert Camoo, and he arrested him!!!! Talk about gonads, "Daddy" may be a little guy, but he's got balls the size of coco nuts!!!!!!

Well it caused a ruckus, I can tell you. There must have been about fifty reporters and photografers, and they were all yelling stuff and popping flashbulbs and carrying on, the jerks! "Daddy" called over a frog policeman and demanded that he take these guys to jail, but the stupid cop didn't even speak English! But finally "Daddy" must have got through to him, because suddenly we were all headed down to the police station. That was when the gooey stuff started to hit the fan, if you know what I mean. Those froggy policemen, they call them John-darns, it turns out they're all Commies (no bull). They were shouting at "Daddy" (in French! arrigant sonsabitches!) and carrying on, and he told them he was going to call the

Marines to come in and declare Marshall Law which he can do. And I told them I was going to call Maurice Chevalier, which I can do, but "Daddy" gave me such a look!

And then they called the American Embassy who sent down someone called the Charge Guy of Fairies, who got Sen. McCarthy (!) on the phone in Washington, and finally they let Kerraway go under his own something or other, but all his books are being consecrated from the libraries and he has a suppena!

Anyway I have to run. Maurice is picking me up later to take me to the Follies Bergeres while "Daddy" is at meeting at the embassy. I'm running out of money so I "lifted" some from "Daddy's" wallet, don't tell!

Love and kisses,

Davey

(ENCRYPTED AND DECODED)
(4/27)
FROM: ALLEN DULLES
TO: ROBERT COHN

WHAT'S YOUR NEPHEW DOING? HAS HE GONE CRAZY?

DULLES

(ENCRYPTED AND DECODED)
(4/27)
FROM: ALLEN DULLES
TO: NICHOLAS CARRAWAY

WHAT ARE YOU GUYS UP TO? A CITIZEN'S ARREST? WERE YOU IN ON THIS? YOU'RE SUPPOSED TO CLEAR ALL PLANS WITH ME BEFORE YOU PUT THEM INTO ACTION. THE FRENCH ARE GOING NUTS! AND HOW THE HELL IS COHN PLANNING TO DECLARE MARTIAL LAW IN FRANCE? STAND BY FOR INSTRUCTIONS. FROM HERE ON, CRUCIAL TO DO EXACTLY AS I SAY.

DULLES

(ENCRYPTED AND DECODED)
(4/27)
FROM: ALLEN DULLES
TO: ROY COHN

DOES THIS HAVE ANYTHING TO DO WITH ELBA? OPERATION CANCELED--DIDN'T YOU GET MEMO? YOU'RE EITHER INSUBORDINATE OR INSANE! WE NEVER HEARD OF YOU. LET ME KNOW IF YOU NEED ANYTHING.

DULLES

(ENCRYPTED AND DECODED)
(4/27)
FROM: NICHOLAS CARRAWAY
TO: ALLEN DULLES

OF COURSE I WASN'T IN ON IT. IT WAS THAT IDIOT COHN. I HAVE NO HANDLE ON THE SITUATION. BUT I CAN TELL YOU THE FRENCH GOVERNMENT IS MAD AS HORNETS, AND THE EMBASSY HERE IS WORKING LIKE HERCULES TO CLEAN UP COHN'S MESS. I HAVE TO TELL YOU, ALLEN, THINGS LOOK VERY DIFFERENT FROM HERE THAN THEY DID BACK IN WASHINGTON. LOOKING AT AMERICA AND AMERICANS FROM A PERSPECTIVE OF NEARLY 4,000 MILES IS NOT UNLIKE THE EXPERIENCE I HAD LOOKING AT LONG ISLAND THROUGH THE BATTERED PRISM OF AN UNDERWOOD TYPEWRITER. THERE'S GREAT AFFECTION, BUT A CERTAIN CHILLING REALIZATION OF DARK THINGS LURKING IN THE SHADOWS. I'M NOT SURE, AS WE SIT IN OUR OAK-PANELED OFFICES IN WASHINGTON, THAT WE'RE AS SENSITIVE TO NUANCE AS WE OUGHT TO BE. I THINK IT MAY BE TIME FOR A WHOLE NEW APPROACH. I SUGGEST WE POSTPONE ANY FURTHER ACTION UNTIL YOU AND I HAVE HAD A CHANCE TO TALK MORE. I CAN COME BACK TO WASHINGTON, BUT NOT FOR A COUPLE OF WEEKS. I HAVE A FEW OBLIGATIONS HERE.

CARRAWAY

4/27/53
FROM: MLLE CHRISTINE JORGENSEN
KEMPINSKI HOTEL
BERLIN

TO: JAKE BARNES
ROYAL HOSPITAL
COPENHAGEN

DAVEY WRITES COHN CITIZENS ARRESTED CARRAWAY IN PARIS STOP DAVEY MOST IMPRESSED BY DADDY STOP DONT THEY REALIZE NO OF COURSE NOT STOP ARRIVING PARIS TONIGHT HOTEL DU LOUVRE. WHEN ARE YOU BACK

LOVE CHRIS

4/28
FROM: ROBERT COHN
WASHINGTON, DC

TO: DAVID SCHINE
HOTEL GEORGE V
PARIS

DAVEY
JORGENSEN AT HOTEL DU LOUVRE STOP MONITOR MAIL FROM BARNES STOP MAY BE SOURCE OF LEAK STOP I WANT TO NAIL THAT BASTARD

ROBERT

4/28
FROM: ROY COHN
HOTEL GEORGE V
PARIS

TO: HON JOSEPH MCCARTHY
RUSSELL SENATE OFFICE BUILDING
WASHINGTON, DC

ARRIVE WASHINGTON 8 A.M. TOMORROW STOP WORK HERE DONE STOP NEXT THE ARMY

COHN

Hotel de l'Odeon

Paris

April 29, 1953

Dear M. Camus:

I am delighted to accept your kind invitation to read tomorrow evening at Shakespeare and Company, if the invitation still stands. I prefer to read selections from Trimalchio rather than the work in progress, which is not nearly ready for the light of day. But I thank you for your interest and encouragement.

Again, for myself and my country, my profoundest apologies for your being caught up in the insanity the other day at Deux Magots. M. Cohn has been summoned back to Washington, and I hope this embarrassing episode will be soon forgotten.

Sincerely,

Nicholas Carraway

Royal Hospital
Copenhagen, Denmark

April 29, 1953

Dear Chris,

Yes, wasn't that a fine mess? All hell breaks loose, and me not in Paris to cover the goddamn story. I always thought I had a nose for news. Just goes to show, you add a new appendage, the others go straight to fuck all!

I figure that yahoo McCarthy was behind it. Or maybe it was just the lackey trying to impress his master, although I would never have credited Cohn with the gonads for a move like that on his own. A citizen's arrest of Nick Carraway! I gather it damned near caused a government crisis. You almost have to give it to the little creep for sheer unmitigated world-class cocked-up showmanship.

Having said that, those sons of bitches make me vomit. They're everything I hate about America (is that your husky contralto in my mind's ear saying, 'Jake, dear, doesn't that mean they're trying to destroy everything you love about America?') All right, and from where I sit, they're doing a damn good job of it. I hear even the Cincinnati Reds are planning to change their name. Well, why the fuck not? There haven't been any reds in Cincinnati since the Palmer Raids.

And is there anyone left to stand up to that mob? Winchell's gone farther to the right than that petrified asshole Ed Sullivan. Even old lefties like my so-called pal Irving Kristol are saying, "Well, you know, there really is a threat."

Yeah, there's a threat all right. Just ask some of the guys who've been driven out of the country. I got a letter from Howard Koch, a writer friend who's on the blacklist--the one they swear doesn't exist. He wrote a movie called Casablanca about ten years ago. No one much remembers it today, but it was a hell of a flick. He's in England now, and I've been telling him he should just stay the hell away from the whole craziness, but he's planning to go back, in spite of the goddamn blacklist.

And then there's Nick. Nick's a decent guy, and I'm glad as hell I've had this chance to get to know him. I guess I can thank McCarthy for that, so I take back all the crap I said about the cocksucker. Well, like the guy in Howard's movie says, everyone in Casablanca has problems. Nick's may work out.

I'd feel a lot better if I were back in Paris. There's something going on--I'll find out soon enough. Nick's coming to Copenhagen to pick me up, and we're going to take a few days for a leisurely drive back to Paris, sampling the local vintages along the way. I'm thinking a little detour might be in order, if you're game. Let's you and me rendezvous in Normandy. I'll have Nick drop me off at a little inn I know near St. Laurent-sur-Mer. I'll check the exact address and cable you with driving instructions. Meet me Thursday next. I was there in '44 covering the invasion, and the place still packs a hell of a goddamn wallop for me.

Now I've got another beachhead to storm.

With love,

Jake (and my new pal, Little Jake)

(COPIED AND FORWARDED BY DIPLOMATIC POUCH FROM ROY COHN TO ROBERT COHN, WASHINGTON DC.)

May 2nd

Uncle Robert,

I'm back in Washington, and damned glad to be here. How'd you like my little Paris surprise?

I thought someone should know this, and frankly, I'm a little hesitant to tell Dulles myself, because he's not going to exactly like it. I think Barnes knows more than he ought to about plans that he ought not to know about. And I'm afraid it was my former friend Davey who's responsible. He's been going all dorky, sneaking around and acting like he thinks he's some kind of a spy. I saw Barnes's name on the phone pad, and when I asked Davey he wouldn't say what it was about, he just looked like a cat who'd swallowed a cloak and dagger. As I said, it's Davey who is responsible. I can assure you I never told Davey anything secret (no bull). It's not like we were in bed together, ha ha.

Maybe you and Aunt Frances could have me over for a home-cooked meal. I'm sick of that frog food!

Your nephew, Roy

To: The Hon. Prescott Bush

5/2/53

Scottie--Dulles getting cold feet. Not the man he was. We'll have to go over him, not through him. If there's a shakeup at the Company and I end up in charge, so be it. If Ike looks weak, a few swift jabs could rattle war hero image, and set stage for a Bush in White House next election. See how chips fall. Meanwhile, need your son to help with a little end around play. Tell George to run all France cables to and from Dulles past me first.

Robbie

From: Hon. Prescott Bush

To: Robert Cohn

5/2/53

Robbie--You get one shot. Then the door closes. I've got plans for that young man, and they don't include any possibility of scandal.

Scottie

JAZZ NOTES FROM AROUND TOWN

by Francis Paudras
May 3, 1953

PARIS--Don't forget to "dig" the magnificent Sidney Bechet as he plays le jazz hot at the Café du Monde.

The always-appealing Blossom Dearie debuts her new ensemble, the Blue Stars, at Caveau de la Huchette.

The legendary American pianist Bud Powell, just returned to Paris from a series of concerts in Sweden and Denmark, played Monday evening at an emotion-charged evening at Shakespeare & Cie honoring the noted American novelist Nicholas Carraway for his heroic stand against McCarthy lackey Roy Cohn. M. Powell will be appearing nightly at Le Bar Negre.

Hotel de l'Odeon

Paris

May 3, 1953

Dear Jake, Father of Contemporary Journalism and Contemporary of Fatherless Journalists,

We miss you here in the Center of the World. Where are you, when all the good stuff's going on?

You'll have heard of my fantastic dust-up with the unspeakable Cohn. As your friend Paudras would put it, "all Paris is talking about l'affaire Carraway." I will save the eyewitness report for when I see you in a few days, but suffice it to say it was a novel and not altogether pleasant experience. Well, but what is a writer about if not experience?

What made it particularly galling was the timing. I was sitting in Deux Magots with Camus, and he was just about to propose. I was like the spinster virgin, fanning myself, with "Yes! and Yes!" rolled up in my tongue, waiting for him to make his declaration. The Camus proposal was an invitation for me to do a reading under his auspices at Shakespeare & Co., but before he could get it said (you know how he hems and pauses) the little rodent Cohn appeared at my elbow, and declared me his prisoner!

The resulting scandale has made me the unlikely hero of the hour in Paris literary circles, and what was, I'm sure, to have been a modest little event with tea sandwiches and lemonade escalated into a Major Event, with a full bar and speeches and testimonials, and even music--what music!--from our friend Mr. Powell, who has just returned to town. Oh, and I read from Trimalchio, and everybody clapped like hell.

I could hardly believe some of the notables who turned out--Camus, of course, and Sartre and de Beauvoir, and Malraux. Picasso was there, and drew a caricature of me on a napkin that I will have to show you. The director Jean Renoir told me he wants to make Trimalchio into a movie with the title of Gatsby le Magnifique. He plans to cast Gerard Philippe in my role (an obvious choice, you'll say,) and Yves Montand as Gatsby, with Jean Gabin as Meyer Wolfsheim. Montand was with him, and could not have looked less impressed. But he has an undeniable magnetism, and I could imagine him in the role of a Gallic version of my tragic gangster.

I handled all of that pretty well, I think. It was later that I got rattled. A teenage French girl came up and told me that she intends to sleep with every famous writer in France before she turns eighteen, and then to write a great novel. Her name was Francoise something--Saggan, I think. She looked me over with a frankness that made me shrivel. She told me that her father absolutely hated ugly people, which meant that he took up with one beautiful empty-headed mistress after another, but she liked clever people. "Of course," she said, "they can't be completely devoid of physical charm. People who resign themselves to the fact that they don't measure up physically seem to me somehow indecent. What are we looking for, if not to please?"

I excused myself and said I had to go to the bathroom, which was not the place most calculated to get me out of a mood of self-doubt as to whether I would measure up to Francoise's standards. I confess I hid out in there. And when I came out, her attention had shifted to Montand.

But I wasn't out of the woods. Next, I was accosted by Simone de Beauvoir, who bore down on me with wolfish eyes that made young Francoise seem like a hamster. "So," she purred, "the paradigm I have never been able to resist ... that classic American species, the self-made leftist writer." She seized me in an intimate grip that robbed me of speech and very nearly of manhood. But at that crucial moment Sartre intervened, and saved what I shall call my bacon.

This time, I ran for the bathroom.

What's wrong with me, Jake? Oak Park was never like this! Was I married too long? Am I just insecure and naïve, or am I really, as I fear, not equipped the way a man ought to be?

I know this is Paris, and I'm a single fellow, and I've gained a certain notoriety, and I should be taking advantage of it, not thinking about one girl all the time. A man has to sow some wild oats, doesn't he? And if I'm afraid of not being enough for a woman, better to find out on someone with whom it won't matter to me so much if I'm found wanting.

This must all seem so juvenile to you. Anyway, other than that I've been working. Writing and eating, tearing it up, and throwing it up. Oh, and in two weeks (!) Girodias is bringing out a new edition of Trimalchio, in his Traveler's Companion series. He's offered me a very handsome advance against royalties, which I may well need, as I don't know how long I'll be keeping my current source of income (which I'll have to tell you about, I suspect you've been wondering.) They call it an advance because they promise it long in advance of delivering the cheque. I expect it will arrive shortly.

Very excited about our trip. Anything I can bring you? Food, money, some of this surplus of women?

Your Devoted Friend,

Nick

5/3/53
Mr. Cohn — The following was intercepted from Barnes in Copenhagen. Do I show it to D.?
GHWB

DULLES - IN POSSESSION OF DOCUMENTATION OF ELBA PLANS. WILL NOT HESITATE TO MAKE PUBLIC IF OPERATION NOT TERMINATED IMMEDIATELY. YOU KNOW I MEAN IT. PLEASE CONFIRM. BARNES

From: Robert Cohn
To: George H. W. Bush

5/3

Show D. nothing. I'll handle this.

C

5/3

Mr. Dulles,
Here's a cable from Barnes. Await instructions.

George H. W. Bush, Communications Center

(ENCRYPTED AND DECODED)
(5/3)
FROM: ALLEN DULLES
TO: IRVING KRISTOL

SEE ATTACHED FROM YOUR PAL BARNES. HAS HE TURNED TRAITOR?

DULLES

(ENCRYPTED AND DECODED)
(5/3)
FROM: I. KRISTOL
TO: A. DULLES

WORSE. HE'S AN IDEALIST.

KRISTOL

(ENCRYPTED AND DECODED)
(5/3)
FROM: ALLEN DULLES
TO: IRVING KRISTOL

WILL BARNES KEEP HIS WORD?

DULLES

(ENCRYPTED AND DECODED)
(5/3)
FROM: I. KRISTOL
TO: A. DULLES

HE ALWAYS HAS.

K

5/3/53
FROM: ROBERT COHN
WASHINGTON, DC

TO: G. DAVID SCHINE
HOTEL GEORGE V
PARIS

DAVEY--GOOD WORK ON LETTER BARNES MUST BE STOPPED STOP ARRIVING PARIS TOMORROW AM STOP HIRE CAR WE'RE GOING TO ST LAURENT SUR MER

ROBBIE

Apartment C
14½ MacDougal Street
New York

May 3, 1953

Darling Nick,

Please listen to the enclosed recording. Mr. Wexler took me into the studio this week, and here is the result. A demo, they call it--a demonstration record. Mr. Wexler wanted to see what I sounded like with real musicians--and what wonderful musicians they were! The pianist is named Red Garland. The bassist, Paul Chambers. The drummer, the sweetest man in the world--next to you, of course--is named Philly Joe Jones. And so complex! If Mr. Wexler hadn't told me to listen to the bass to get the beat, I would have been lost completely. Then for the instrumental break, he used a wonderful young tenor saxophone player named David Newman, who everyone--except me, of course--calls Fathead!!!! Can you imagine??? I hope you'll listen to my second chorus of "Lover Come Back," after David's instrumental part. After listening to his improvisation, I felt like I understood the melody so much better.

"Lover Come Back." It could be our song, couldn't it? And when you turn the record over, you'll hear the song that I insisted on doing, and you can guess why: "April in Paris."

Much much love, my dearest man,

Ronnie

(GIVEN BY HAND TO GEORGE H. W. BUSH FOR ENCRYPTION AND TRANSMISSION)
5/3/53
FROM: ALLEN DULLES
TO: GEN. RAOUL SALAN

CALLING OFF OPERATION ELBA. TOO RISKY AT THIS TIME. REPEAT, ELBA IS OVER. AWAIT INSTRUCTIONS.

DULLES

5/3/53
Mr. Cohn - Dulles is pulling the plug on Elba — see attached cable draft.
GHWB

5/3/53

George--Thanks for the heads up. Keep letting me know everything that goes out on this matter--BEFORE you send it. Substitute this message:

Gen. Salan--Stand by for signal. Coded message in Barnes Door Thursday Herald Tribune. Dulles

(ENCRYPTED AND DECODED)
(5/3)
FROM: ROBERT COHN
TO: NICK CARRAWAY

DUCKS IN ROW. TOP SECRET INSTRUCTIONS FROM DULLES: USE YOUR BARNES COLUMN TO RUN THIS PIECE. IMPORTANT: NO CHANGES!

FRANCE REMAINS IN AN UPROAR, WITH CIVIL UNREST SWEEPING THE COUNTRY, AND FROM WHERE I SIT, THE FRENCH GOVERNMENT IS DOING NOTHING. THE SITUATION CRIES OUT FOR A FIRM HAND--CURFEWS, A STATE OF EMERGENCY. THE RECENT UNREST IN ALGIERS HAS PRODUCED LAWS IN FRANCE TO DEAL WITH THIS STATE OF AFFAIRS. BUT ENFORCING THEM IS A MATTER OF WILL, AND I HAVEN'T SEEN ANYTHING FROM THIS COUNTRY'S CURRENT BUNCH OF COOKIE CUTTER POLITICOS THAT SHOWS ANY BACKBONE.

IT'S A SURE SIGN OF A DEGENERATE CULTURE. LAW AND ORDER HAVE GONE INTO THE TOILET. IF I WERE A PARISIAN SHOPKEEPER, I'D BE BOARDING UP MY STOREFRONT RIGHT AROUND NOW. THE STREETS ARE GOING TO BE FULL OF PEOPLE WHO ARE NO RESPECTERS OF PROPERTY RIGHTS, AND MORE WHO ARE SIMPLY FED UP WITH A GOVERNMENT OF SPINELESS CLOWNS.

THE REAL DANGER, OF COURSE, IS THAT THE COMMUNISTS WILL TAKE ADVANTAGE OF THIS SITUATION TO SEIZE POWER IN A CITY THAT'S ALREADY FAR TOO COMMIE-FRIENDLY, AND THEN

GOODBYE TO A ONCE-PROUD FREEDOM-LOVING COUNTRY. YOUR CORRESPONDENT HAS HAD PLENTY OF EXPERIENCE WITH THESE COMMIES. DUE TO A MISUNDERSTANDING INVOLVING THE INEPT GOVERNMENT AND KEYSTONE GENDARMERIE, AND SOME NONSENSE ABOUT A BIT OF LITERARY JUVENILIA THAT I'D LONG SINCE FORGOTTEN, I BECAME THE OVERNIGHT DARLING OF THE PINKO SET. WELL, I'M HERE TO TELL YOU, THESE ARE THE SORT OF PSEUDO-INTELLECTUALS WHO ARE AS LIKELY AS NOT TO LATCH ONTO JERRY LEWIS AS THEIR NEXT CULTURAL DARLING.

THE FRENCH GOVERNMENT, IF IT SURVIVES, WILL HAVE A LOT TO ANSWER FOR. BUT THEN, FRENCH GOVERNMENTS COME AND GO THESE DAYS LIKE THE TOURISTS WHO VISIT THE EIFFEL TOWER. AND IF THIS SITUATION CONTINUES, THERE WON'T BE A LOT OF THOSE.

AS FOR ME, I'M READY FOR A VACATION FAR AWAY FROM HERE. BACK IN AMERICA. MAYBE OUT WEST, WHERE THE ASPENS WILL ALREADY BE TURNING. THEY TURN IN CLUSTERS, BECAUSE THEIR ROOTS CONNECT THEM. I NEED TO GET BACK TO WORK--AND LIFE.

REMEMBER, CARRAWAY, DULLES EMPHASIZES NO CHANGES!

ROBERT COHN

Hotel de l'Odeon

Paris

May 3

Dearest Ronnie,

I've just gotten the damnedest message from a man I respect very much, a top man in the Administration, with whom I've been involved in the service of our country. He wants me to use my guest turn in Jake's Trib column to plant a piece of muckraking garbage I'm to present as my own words. His orders are to run it exactly as he sent it to me. It's incendiary, it's insulting, and some of it's incomprehensible--aspens turning in clusters because their roots connect them??? What the devil does that mean??? I have a terrible feeling it's a coded message.

Dammit, Ronnie, I don't know what to do. Loyalties! My first loyalty is to my country and my government. But what about my loyalty to Jake? If I betray his trust by putting this poison into the paper, he'll never speak to me again. It will make for a very uncomfortable drive down from Copenhagen, if he even still wants me to meet him after this.

And Ronnie, what about you? How will you feel about a man who could do this? I'll have betrayed you too. But the inescapable fact is: I can't betray my country.

I'm going out for a walk. And then I guess I'll take this column over to the Trib, where I'll deposit this letter to you in their overnight pouch to New York. Instant communication. One of the perquisites of newspaper life.

Love,

Nick

17 rue du Dragon
Paris, France

May 4, 1953

M. Barnes,

I received a message from M. Bud Powell, and met him as instructed at Le Bar Negre. He handed me a packet of documents from you, which he had smuggled into Paris hidden inside his piano.

I made the mistake of giving him the payment you had promised while I was still inspecting the contents of the packet. When I looked up he had disappeared.

I found M. Bud in a disreputable boite, which indulges the unfortunate and illegal French passion for absinthe. The green poison had already worked its mischief, and to my mortification he initially confused me with M. Hugues Panassié, the noted jazz critic and moldy fig, enemy of all that is innovative.

I managed to break through his phantasm, and you can imagine my joy when not only did he recognize me, but he importuned me to stay and listen to a new composition.

Of course, I had no choice. M. Barnes, you of all men must understand. And you can but imagine what it was like, sitting in a corner of this filthy dive, surrounded by prostitutes, pochards on the verge of delirium tremens, incautious tourists and predatory loubards, and three mangy cats, listening to a new work of unparalleled genius. M. Bud began with a simple, haunting melody that resolved itself into a minor 7th chord, at once jarring and soothing, and moved into a string of contrapuntally playful arpeggios, beginning with the blues and extending into the territory of fugue ...

But I digress. I was able to convince M. Bud to come home with me, where I gave him a cup of hot tea and put him to bed. I left, locking the door behind me to keep him safe. Then I went to find M. Carraway.

At the Herald-Tribune I was informed that he had already dropped off his column. I tried his hotel. The concierge told me that he had returned to the Herald-Tribune. I understood that the errand was growing urgent, so I stopped for no more than a moment to look in on M. Bud before making a line of bees for the newspaper office.

I found M. Carraway in the composing room, engaged in a heated argument with the compositeur. I approached him with the packet you had entrusted to me.

"M. Carraway," I said breathlessly, "I bring you a packet of information from M. Barnes himself! He instructed me to inform you that you should read it before writing your column."

"Thank you," he replied, "but I have just completed my column."

"Too late!" interjected M. le compositeur. "The earlier version you submitted has been set in type!"

M. Carraway turned on the man, and there was steel in his voice.

"Listen to me," he snapped. "You will tear out this column, and replace it with the one I give you now! The earlier version was a mistake, and its publication would dishonor Mr. Barnes. Nothing must go into this newspaper that will do discredit to Jake Barnes. Do you understand me?"

M. Barnes, you should have seen him! His resolve was like a furnace, and the poor man melted before him. Then M. Carraway turned to me, and these were his words:

"Tell Jake thanks," he said, "but I'm not going to look at the documents, whatever they are. I'll do this my way."

I picked up the packet and brought it home with me, where it rests on my bedside table, as M. Bud sits at the upright piano in the corner, putting the finishing touches on his new composition, "Hallucination."

Sincerely,

Francis Paudras

(ENCRYPTED AND DECODED)
(5/4/53)
FROM: NICHOLAS CARRAWAY
TO: ALLEN DULLES

I COULDN'T USE THE COLUMN YOU SENT ME. I'M SORRY. BUT I JUST DON'T BELIEVE ANYMORE. I'M THROUGH WITH ALL THAT. I'LL ALWAYS CONSIDER YOU A FRIEND. BUT THIS IS A CLOSED BOOK IN MY LIFE. THIS WILL BE MY LAST COMMUNICATION TO YOU THROUGH CHANNELS.

NICK

Atlantic Hotel
Hamburg, Germany

May 4, 1953

Jake, you dear old bear,

You must be proud of your friend this morning. The way he socked it to McCarthy, and "the danger to the American soul, if our government continues its present course of sacrificing our humanity and the core of our democracy at the altar of cold war expediency." Wow!

I was interested to note, though, that he didn't use any of the documents I'd liberated courtesy of Clyde Tolson, and delivered to you. Did you decide not to give them to him?

For the first time since my operation, I've been experiencing phantom limb syndrome. And I don't mean a pain or an itch, either. Well, I suppose you could call it a sort of an itch.

I don't like it much. I wanted to get rid of that thing. I don't want it suddenly getting all hard and throbbing on me, and it not even there. What makes it bearable is knowing where it is now. And wondering if what I'm feeling at those moments is what you're feeling. Phantom limb syndrome or sympathetic desire? Either way, I want to put it to rest. And something tells me that in order for that to be buried once and for all, it has to be buried inside me.

By the pricking of my thumbs,
Something wicked this way comes.

And the sooner the better.

Oh, Jake, we're going to have such a damn fine time together!

Love,

Christine

From the desk of:

Allen Dulles

By Messenger
5/5/1953

To: George H. W. Bush

I want to know two things. First, this cable from Carraway, what the hell is he talking about? I didn't send him a column. Who did? Second, who have you been conspiring with? You've got a future in this organization, Bush, but you've been playing a dangerous game. I'll tell you something--your father can't help you. Prescott Bush is never going to be president. But remember this--his son could be, and his son's sons, if you're willing to learn where the true power lies, and who to listen to, and how to take orders.

And remember this. If someone can't help you, it's time to dump him, even if he is your father.

Come straight to my office on receipt of this. Immediately. And talk to no one. Especially no one named Robert Cohn.

Dulles

14½ MacDougal Street
New York

May 5, 1953

My dearest Nick,

I sat down to write you a letter in which I was going to tell you that whatever you decided, it would be all right with me. I know that you've devoted so much of your life to an ideal of America. I know, because I grew up the same way. I didn't serve in a war, of course, but as a little girl I felt like I was part of it, saving my little cans of bacon fat and balls of tinfoil, and planting my little victory garden. I used to salute every morning when I came out to water my string beans and radishes. But that was Winnetka, in what feels like another lifetime.

New York can change you. It certainly changed me. But I was writing you to tell you that you didn't have to change for me to love you. I know that first and foremost, you're an honorable man, and whatever you decided, it would be honest and principled. First thing this morning I went out and picked up the Paris Herald Tribune. When I saw the column you'd written, I just melted. I was actually crying into my espresso at the Café Figaro. (I go there a lot; it's just down the block from me, and the walls are all covered in French newspapers, so it makes me feel somehow closer to you.)

There's a spring warmth in the air that's found its way even into the concrete canyons of New York, but that doesn't explain the way I felt. I was warm and tingly all over. I had to take several deep breaths before I could even go back to focusing my eyes on what you'd written. You are my hero. If it had been you sitting with me at that moment, instead of just your words on a printed page, I would have jumped right over the table and smothered you with kisses. Oh, Nick, I do want to smother you with kisses. I want to hold you in my arms. You must feel it too. Say you do.

But when will we ever see each other? I loved what you said at the end of your column, about finding what you had come to think of as a realer America than you'd ever known in the musical voice of Bud Powell and the expatriate American voices of musicians like Sidney Bechet and Blossom Dearie. But does this mean ... you're never coming home? I miss you so much, my darling, it makes me ache.

Love,

Ronnie

Maurice Chevalier

5/5/1953
By messenger

General Salan:

The message in today's column has been cleverly concealed, but it appears to be embedded in the list of obscure names at the end of the column--Bud Powell, Sidney Bechet, Blossom Dearie. If these are American entertainers, I am a resistance fighter. None of them has ever appeared at the Folies Bergère, I can assure you. And that last name on the list is surely the coded reference, to message 273: We look forward to the spring, when we take our loved ones to see the cherry blossoms open along the Potomac.

Translation: Forget France. Devote all your efforts to suppressing those towel-headed colonials in Algiers. Be as brutal as possible to the bastards.

Vive la Falange,

Maurice Chevalier

5/6/53

FROM: NICHOLAS CARRAWAY
HOTEL DE L'ODEON
PARIS

TO: JAKE BARNES
UNIVERSITY CLINIC
COPENHAGEN

ARRIVE COPENHAGEN TOMORROW STOP BE PACKED
AND READY TO ROLL STOP NICK

Jake Barnes
Copenhagen, Denmark
May 6, 1953

Dear Chris,

Nick did me proud. He found that one true sentence, and went on from there.

I did send him the documents. I wasn't going to. I used them as leverage on that bastard Dulles, and in return, I told him they'd go no farther than me. But I started getting a strange feeling in the old short hairs. There was a tap on my phone, and I'm pretty sure somebody was reading my mail. So I decided to let Nick decide what to do with the documents. And as you can see, he went his own way.

It felt like a valedictory, didn't it? Disillusionment can set in hard, once it sets in. I don't know if our boy is ever going back to America. Well, I know what that feels like, don't I?

Sympathetic desire, eh? It could be. I've been getting those same feelings too ... the old pneumatic pump is working the way it oughta. Pending the real test.

Nick is picking me up in the morning, and we'll be heading south. Get ready for the corrida!

Love and anticipation,

Jake

May 8, 1953

My dear Carraway,

A brilliant article. You succinctly captured the existential failure of the nascent American empire. I hope it will be the first of many. I would like to see you writing a regular column for Libération. Say the word and I will approach the editor.

Camus

United States Information Agency
20 rue Lacepede, Paris 5e, FRANCE

May 10, 1953

Dear Ronnie,

I returned to Paris this afternoon to find your wonderful letter and a parcel from you at the hotel. A letter from you is always occasion for excitement--but a parcel! I tore it open with impatient fingers to find your record (demo, is that what you call it?) inside.

Of course I don't have a record player, but there's one at the USIA library, and that is where I have been ever since (note the liberated stationary). I have been tucked away in the audio booth for the last three hours listening to you sing "Lover Come Back" and "April in Paris" over and over again, and I still can't believe it. My God, Ronnie, where did it come from? You always had a voice, but I swear, hearing you do the show's theme song, "Snicklepoo and Me and You," never prepared me for where you've gone with it. There are emotions threaded through your delivery that I don't think I ever felt until I heard you sing these songs. I feel almost criminal now, locking you into that kiddie show for three years when there was this *artist* waiting to burst out! My God, Ronnie--my God!

Time and distance are measures I can't quite put into perspective these days. I feel I've been gone for years, not months. The distance between us seems more like light years than the few paltry thousand miles that either of us could annihilate in a matter of hours with an airplane ticket. What's been happening to us, Ronnie? Is there anything left in you of the pigtailed young woman I hired in Chicago? Is there anything left in me of the pompous stuffed shirt who pushed that contract across the desk at you?

I wonder this because I want desperately to see you, Ronnie, and at the same time nothing I've ever contemplated has scared me more. I keep telling myself I don't really know this girl--this woman--and as the song goes, how can you lose what you've never owned? But I feel as if I can lose, and lose a lot, and it may be more painful than I'm ready to risk.

There are many reasons for this fear--our ages, of course, and habits, and tastes, and experiences, and a jester's pouch of other reasons. But I'd be lying to myself and to you if I didn't admit that there is one issue that scares me more than all the others. It's a small thing, in a way, and yet it casts a shadow I may not be able to overcome. It seems to have been a problem in my marriage, although one I was never aware of until the end, and since, in which time Marjorie has not stinted in drawing it to my attention. It's a thing I could never address in a letter, and yet that may be the only way to do it, because I know I'll never be able to broach it in person.

So here's what I'm going to do. I've just returned to Paris after my drive down from Denmark with Jake. I dropped him off yesterday at a little inn along the Normandy coast--I'm pretty sure he had an assignation lined up, but he was being damned mysterious about it.

In fact, he still hasn't told me what his business in Copenhagen was, but I have the feeling he was getting hold of something important. There's a different quality to him, Ronnie, a kind of swagger I've never seen in Jake before, and I don't yet know what to make of it. But that's for another letter.

What I'm going to do, now, is to tear out a few pages of my journal from the trip, and include them here. I wrote these entries for myself, so they address the subject with a lack of self-consciousness that I could never manage if I were telling the story directly to you.

There are words in it I would never use in front of a young lady, and I am mortified to put them in front of you. But I feel this is something too important to avoid. If this offends you, I understand. I won't expect to hear from you for a while; and if, after some time, you feel like picking up our correspondence again as if nothing had happened, and keeping the distance and relationship between us as it has been, a sort of confessional exchange between a middle-aged man and his young protégé, I will willingly slip back into that harness.

So--read it, and if necessary, weep. The reassurance Jake offers me here on this matter of my agonizing uncertainty is not the point. He calls it a matter of perspective. His is one thing, Marjorie's another. The one that will matter is yours.

With love,
Nick

From my diary —

May 6 - On the train to Copenhagen

On my way to Copenhagen to meet Jake. He still hasn't volunteered anything about the purpose of his trip, and unless he brings it up, I'll respect that. But he has been very urgent that I come up to meet him so we can drive back to Paris together. Once I learned that he'd liked my column, I didn't need much convincing.

Jake has arranged the hire of a car. I am to pick him up tomorrow at the University. We'll wend our way down through Germany and the Pays-Bas + maybe carve off a little taste of Belgium, partaking of the local wines + the fat of the land, talking about writing, and having a rare old time.

After the tumult of the past weeks, it will be both a pleasure and a relief to be away from Paris, adrift like Huck + Jim on a river of idleness, letting the current of conversation carry us where it will. I know I can learn a lot from Jake. Rediscovering myself as a writer, being taken up by the Paris literary world, has been the most exhilarating experience of my life. I feel invigorated + intoxicated. It's as if someone has reattached my male equipment after years of my not noticing the stuff was missing.

Speaking of which, one of the highlights of my evening at Shakespeare + Co came after the reading when de Beauvoir backed me against a bookcase + grasped me firmly by the crotch while looking me over like a woman choosing a cut of meat at the butcher's. I was at a loss for words, and might have lost more than that. Happily, Sartre came by and said something sharply to her in French, and she released me with a very Gallic shrug. I gave him an embarrassed nod of thanks, and he returned a sardonic smile.

Am I just enjoying the celebrity? Or is it the writing I crave? And can I still do it? By the time Keats was my age, he'd been dead for 30 yrs. But then, so have I.

May 7

Picked up the car. It's a pre-war Renault convertible, the color of egg yolk. Cloth top resists all efforts to put it up. We can only hope it doesn't rain. The thing runs, anyway, and the evil garage man who gave me the keys swore it has a full tank of gas – no way of telling, as the gauge is busted. Sitting outside the Royal Hospital waiting for Jake. Impatient to start the trip....

May 7- night

Jake came down to the car – bounded, you might almost say – tossed his suitcase into the boot, clapped me on the back, + sang out "Come on, Nicko me boy, let's roll!"

We sped along through the Danish countryside, stopped for a late lunch at an inn where there was no English and little French spoken, but where we nevertheless managed to get a good meal of very fresh monkfish + a crisp white wine.

Clouds were gathering in the west as we left the inn. We wrestled with the soft top, + managed to rip it clean off its rusted moorings. We laughed hilariously, + left it propped up as a shrine on the side of the road. Jake was in exuberant spirits, which even the drenching rain didn't seem to dampen. Nor did the discovery of the garage man's treachery, when we ran out of gas. I was able to wave down a truck + get a lift to a gas station, but we lost a few hours + have wound up stopping here on the island of Funen for the night.

Found a wonderful inn with sloping thatched roofs + ivy on the walls + red + white flowers in neat beds + windowboxes. We were able to change into some dry clothes and tuck into an excellent dinner while management arranged our wet things by the kitchen fireplace. Jake flirting broadly with the innkeeper's wife as she served us, which amused her but not the innkeeper. I've not seen this randy side of Jake before. He seems positively giddy. Maybe it's the wine, or the Danish climate.

May 8 —

Jake's asleep. I can't sleep. What a day!

Made our way by ferry to the mainland, and tootled south, keeping to the coast + crossing into Germany by lunchtime. Jake entertained me with a rollicking rendition of "Barnacle Bill the Sailor", trilling the maiden's falsetto parts + growling Bill's bass parts, + howling with laughter. It was hard not to be infected by his mood, and after we stopped at a farmhouse + Jake disappeared inside + emerged with a basket of bottles of local wine, it became progressively easier to join in the hilarity.

After a few bottles I needed a piss. We were on a straight stretch of road without a farmhouse in sight.

"I don't know if I can hold it," I said.

"Why hold it?"

"Well — but out here?"

"Why the fuck not? Anybody coming,

we'll see 'em two kilometers away, if that's what worries you." He flung open the passenger door. "Tell you the truth, I could use a leak myself."

I have always been a physically modest man. In the years since I made the transition to long pants I don't think I have relieved myself outdoors more than a handful of times – if I may be forgiven the phrasing. I didn't play sports at Yale, and managed to avoid entirely the naked, towel-snapping camaraderie of the locker room.

I had never even been to the men's room with Jake. I preferred it that way – I tend to use a stall if one is available – and I always thought Jake preferred his privacy as well.

So it startled the hell out of me when Jake strode around the car + took up a position next to me, + began unbuttoning his pants.

"It's not going to do you any good in there," he chaffed me as I hesitated with my hands suspended in front of my fly. "Come on, Nick, don't be an old woman. It's just us and the daisies!"

There are moments when doing something embarrassing is less mortifying than prim refusal. And so I found myself pissing onto

German soil, side by side with Jake. I couldn't resist a sidelong peek. To my surprise and relief his penis looked perfectly normal.

"For distance!" Jake challenged. I raised up + sent a vigorous stream raining on an anthill some four or five feet away. Jake's effort fell short.

"I haven't done this since I was a kid in the cornfields," I laughed.

Jake finished, and flicked. My effort continued a few moments longer, and I was aware of his eyes watching me with unembarrassed frankness.

"She's crazy," he said.

"Beg your pardon?"

"That wife of yours. Nothing wrong with the size of your cock. Maybe not quite as big as mine...." (here he drew his forward + twisted it between his thumb + forefinger with a pleased smile). "But hell, nothing to be ashamed of either. She's jerking your chain."

"Why would she say it, then?"

"She wants to put you out of business. That's it, pure and simple."

"I don't know. I can't tell."

"You're fine," he said, tucking himself back in. "It's the perspective, Nick. It's foreshortening, from the angle you look at it. It's a swell cock, Nicko. Any woman would be pleased as punch with it."

"You're sure?"

"Trust me," he said. "I've made a study of these things."

Jake Barnes
Saint-Laurent-sur-Mer

May 11

Dear Nick,

Into each life a little shit must fall. You will not believe what's gone on since you so blithely dropped me off at the shore a few days ago.

You'll have guessed that my rendezvous was with a lady. There are ramifications and implications and complications and sidebars that I may tell you about someday, but not now. When you're older. Suffice it to say I was looking forward with uncommon anticipation to getting laid, and so was the lady.

She never arrived. I waited at the Auberge Aubier until close to sunset, and then I liberated a bottle of whiskey from the bar and walked down to Omaha Beach. I had not been there in almost ten years. It was a warm evening and it was very fine outside and there were smells of cooking from the houses and the whiskey burned and it tasted good even if the lady wasn't there.

But the beach was not empty. It was alive with soldiers who jumped off landing craft with their rifles held over their heads and struggled through the surf and up onto sand that was churning with bombs and mortar shells. I could smell the explosives and hear their thunder and feel the impact of the shocks of the explosions and hear the shouts of the men and their screams. They were there, and they were real, and I was the ghost among them.

I sat on a dune and watched the troops storm the beach, and watched the assault, and felt the shells and the bombs exploding around them and all around me, and I drank the whiskey I had brought with me and I thought about the lady who had not arrived, and I wondered what had happened to her and why the bombs and the whiskey were not having any effect on me.

A man was walking toward me across the sand. He wore a hat, and a trench coat that was belted around the middle. He did not look very much different than he had looked thirty years ago, except that he had not worn the hat and the trench coat then. "Hello Robert," I said. "What brings you here?"

"Hello, Jake." Robert Cohn sat down on the dune beside me. "I've come to take you down."

"Well, have a drink."

Cohn took the bottle and drank, and I noticed that the assault had ended and the soldiers were gone and the beach was empty and quiet again.

"Look out there," he said. "That's Africa."

"Where?"

He pointed out to sea.

"No," I said, "that's New York. Africa's down there to the left, past Spain."

"Well, that's where you're going. Africa."

"I can't, Robert. I've got a date with a lady." I took the bottle back. "We'll go shooting in Africa some other time."

"There'll be shooting," he said, "but I'm not going with you. I'm sending you." He took his right hand out of the pocket of the trench coat and there was a gun in it. It was a MAS 50, a French Army pistol. "It's all arranged, Jake. I'm delivering you to a guy who recruits for the French Foreign Legion. You'll be in Algiers in a couple of days. Sorry. You're getting to be too big a problem."

The barrel of the gun made a short arc toward my head and everything went black.

I woke up in the dark and I found that my hands were tied behind my back and my ankles were bound too, and I was in a small confined space. I heard voices.

"Well look who's here." It was Cohn. "Who's your lady friend, Davey?"

"Hello Robert. This is Christine Jorgensen."

"The famous Christine Jorgensen."

"Where is he?" It was the voice of the famous Christine Jorgensen.

"Where is whom?"

"Who," Chris corrected.

There was a gag in my mouth, but the tape had slipped and I spat it out. "I'm in here," I said. I wasn't sure where in here was.

"Jake? You're in the boot?"

"Hard to say."

"Really, Mr. Cohn!" Chris sounded indignant. She sounded like my mother when somebody farted. Chris was a real lady.

I heard a sharp rapping over my head. "Open this trunk immediately!"

A key rasped in a lock, and the lid of the trunk swung up. There was Chris. She looked beautiful. Cohn stood behind her, and behind him off to the left was Davey Schine, looking pale and scared.

"These European cars aren't as roomy as the American models," Cohn said. "It may get a little tight in there." He gave Chris a shove and she tumbled in on top of me into the trunk. The lid slammed shut.

"Hello Jake."

Her mouth was very near mine, and I kissed her. "Hello Chris."

The motor of the car started, and then it stopped. We could hear Cohn's voice, and then Schine's. They were talking, or they were arguing, it was hard to tell.

"Is this the place you wrote me about?" Chris asked.

"No, it's up the beach a bit. It is not very big, but it's bigger than this."

"I was going to rescue you, but I'm not used to the high heels yet."

"Don't worry about it," I said.
I see I'm writing a novel. I hadn't meant

to, but it started coming out that way. I just wrote that one true sentence, and then I went on from there. It's all your fault, Nick. It must be catching, this literary bug of yours. Take two slugs of gin and call me in the morning.

Anyway, here's what happened. All very dramatic and exciting, but not much to it really. If you don't count the gun.

And I don't count the gun. Not really. The Mas 50 is a Browning single-action with a slide-mounted safety. Cohn had some trouble with the safety, so I was able to conk him over the head with the tire iron when he opened the trunk. Chris had obligingly sawed my restraints with her nail file.

We got Cohn trussed up with the rope and gagged with Chris's nylons, and we tucked him into our old quarters. Schine knew where Cohn had set up the contact with the Foreign Legion guy, and he and Chris assured me Davey was on our side now. So I gave him the keys to Cohn's rental car and told him to deliver the package. I told him to tell the guy to make sure they keep the gag in. Tell him this Barnes guy is delusional and more than nine-tenths wacko, but he'll be a hell of a fighter once you get him to Algiers. Schine took the car and pointed it toward Marseilles. I took Mlle. Chris's arm, and pointed her toward the inn. A curtain of decency descends over what followed.

Your old pal unt lit'ry mentor and guide through life,

Jake

Mars Say

May 14

Dear Roy,

Boy, your uncle is crazy! And so are you, for that matter. All you Cohns are nutso! Look, you better get me out of the army, or I've got some things I could tell that a Few People might be intersted in.

You'll be intersted to know that your Uncle Robert has joined the French Foreign Legion. I played a small part in his decision. Well, maybe not so small. But he had it coming. You know what he did to me?

So he asked me to hire a car and pick him up at the Aura Lee Airport in Paris and he said we were going to go on a road trip to this place called St. Lawrence and stop Barnes. So I picked him up. He was kind of spazzing out, you know, and talking a mile a minnet. So we drove a while, and I guess he thought I had a map but I didn't have any map. I mean why would I have a map?

So he got all in a conniption and then he told me to stop at this little gas station where they don't even sell gas they sell essence if you can beleve it, and not cheap! And he told me go in and get a map and I told him you speaka da frog you getta da map. So he gets all bitchy but he gets out and he goes inside and he's in there a long time and finally he comes out and he doesn't have a map. He says they didn't have a map, but he got instructions. Okay.

So off we go again and he keeps telling me okay take a right here, and take a left there, and on and on, and he falls asleep, and next thing you know we're in this town and there's a cathedral and your uncle is saying so that's Rooawn the famous Cathedral of Rooawn and Davey my lad it would be good for you to see it because it's very famous and Monay painted it. So we get out and it turns out it's not Rooawn, its fucking Orleans, where Joan of Ark and Louis Armstrong come from, and which is in a hundred percent the wrong direction.

So we had to turn around and head the other way, and boy was your uncle pissed, but he couldn't make it out to be my fault, even tho he tried! And when I asked him about stopping Barnes, I mean stopping him how, he got all silent with me.

So anyway we lost a day, and we wound up having to spend the night in this jerkwater town on route, in this little dump where they only had one room and it had a double bed! So we had fun anyway, but in the morning your uncle gets all weird on me, and he tells me he wants to do this thing where he ties me up, you know, like when we do that Gulliver thing? Well so anyways I say sure, and he ties me to the bed, and then he stuffs my underpants (the purple ones) in my mouth, and then he grabs his bag and says "So long, Davey," and out he goes!

Okay, I mean I like games. But after a couple of hours I'm starting to think maybe this ain't no game! So I start struggling and thumping the bed and trying to spit out the goddamn underpants, but I'm not getting anywhere and nobody seems to notice except once I heard someone yell up something in French that who knows what the fuck it meant but probly shut up. And then a while later the maid sticks her head in the room and sees me spreadeagled on the bed in the buff, and she just kinda shrugs and shuts the door!

So I'm lying there trying to figure out what the fuck to do, and I here a car pull up outside, and I here this voice say "Excuse me, parley-voo Anglay?" And I think holy crap I know that voice! And I make a mighty goddamn effort and I get the undies out of my mouth and I scream "Christine!"

And it <u>is</u> Christine, you know, my friend I told you about that used to be a guy, I mean what are the fucking odds, right? So she gets me untied and I put my clothes on. And what do you think? It turns out she's on her way to St. Lawrence too, which is how she came to be on that little podunk road in that little podunk town and stopped at that little podunk joint to ask directions. And wait a minnet, you think that's weird? Guess who she was going to St. Lawrence to meet? Jake Barnes!

So I told her about your Uncle Robert and stopping Barnes, and man, she may not have been a girl long, but she can sure scream like one! So we piled into her car and took off in the direction they pointed us. We got to St. Lawrence about sunset, which is not a great time to be driving there because you are looking right into the goddamn sun the whole way. And we pull up to the beach and there's my car, the one I hired, and there's your doofus Uncle Robert.

And it turns out he's got Barnes in the trunk and next thing you know he's got Christine in there too! So he tells me to go get in the car, and boy, I'm shaking by now, because he's already left me tied up once today. So there's this pistol on the seat, one of those neat French Army jobs, and I take my gum and I wedge it under the safety.

And then Robert gets in and he picks up the gun and he starts up the car and he says okay, Davey, I'll take care of you later, which doesn't sound so good to me. And he hands me this piece of paper and he says okay this is where we're going to Mars Say and this is the guy from the French Foreign Legion we're going to meet, and you study these directions careful, you little cocksucker, and if you get us lost again I'll have your nuts. He could charm the little birds out of the trees, your uncle.

And he tells me there's a sonofabitch I've done some business with, Aly Khan, married to Rita Hayworth. A real hardass, used to be an officer in the Legion. Those Arab Muslims know how to keep their people in line, not like Mossydick and those bleeding heart democracy cunts. We could learn from 'em. Pick your nose, they cut off your finger. Aly will make a call, make sure Barnes gets personal attention.

So I ask him what about Christine, and he kind of laughs and says the notorious Christine Jorgensen, do you have any idea what some of those whorehouses in Mars Say would pay for her?

So I have the feeling that if we get started I am so screwed, so I say wait a second, I think I heard something back there, and he says what, and I say I don't know but I think you better check. So he curses and stops the motor and gets out with his gun and goes back to check, and I'm gonna slide over as soon as he's out and drive off like a bat outta hell, but shit he takes the fucking keys!

And then I here something that sounds like what the, and then umnph, and I get out and there's your Uncle Robert stretched out on the ground and Barnes climbing out of the trunk with a goddamn tire iron in his hand and blood in his eye. But Christine God bless her tells him no no, Daveys with us, which you can believe it I was!

So we tie Robert up and stuff him in the trunk, and I tell Barnes about where Robert was going to deliver him to this French Foreign Legion guy, and Barnes kind of smiles. And your uncle says no wait, Jake, don't be crazy, and Barnes says what the hell, Robert, what the hell.

Robert starts yelling, and Christine takes off her nylons and shoves them in his mouth, and Barnes slams down the lid, and hands me the car keys. And he tells me they're expecting Barnes, Davey, you take 'em Barnes.

And I did. I drove like hell down all the way to Mars Say and found the guy down at the waterfront and the last time I saw your uncle he was being loaded onto a freighter. So listen Roy, I think you and me should call it a day. That stuff's okay when you're a kid fooling around, but I'm going to find me a girl and settle down and do something serious with my life. I'm thinking of going into the movies. Anyway I'm sure as hell not going into the Army, so you get that squared away, okay, for old times sake? That way all our little secrets can stay our little secrets.

Your pal,

Davey

May 17

Lady B--

Well, I never thought I'd be writing you about this, although I imagined doing it with you often enough. Hell, I imagined doing it often enough. But here's the scoop. I'm all there now, and it works. It goes up and down. I could change a tire with it. Better than that, I can do what it's designed for. Have done it. The old in and out. Well, I am here to tell you, that's exactly how it works. In. And out. And in. And out. And in ...

Yeah, yeah, you know all about it. But here's the catch, your ladyship. You don't. You don't know a damn thing about it. Nothing can be sole or whole that has not been rent. Now I am the king of the cats.

And one more thing, milady. I'm glad it wasn't you.

Formerly yours,

Jake

Mlle. Christine Jorgensen
Dover Inn
Dover, England

May 17, 1953

Dear Davey,

Good luck with staying out of the army. I hope Roy and the Senator can fix it for you, although frankly, I wouldn't count on either of those two to find a giraffe in a broom closet.

Meanwhile, I know you're wondering--what happened after you left for Marseilles? How did it go? Well, it went ... and went ... and went. And was divine.

Hard as I know it is for you to believe, my adorable little hormonal handful of horny youth, I didn't just undergo this major surgery in order to try out some new sex positions. Not that I'm saying that would be a bad thing. After all, it's basically why Jake had his operation, and I'm so glad that he did.

No, there was much more to it than that, and I know you're not the slightest bit interested in any of the rest of it. So ... it was lovely. Jake was the right man for me in so many ways. We talked, and we drank, and we took our clothes off, which was not quite the easiest thing for either of us. We felt like prepubescent kids. There was a lot of looking, and a lot of touching, gingerly at first. And when it happened, I felt somehow as though I'd been made whole, for the first time. As though for the first time that thing actually fit me.

I don't know that there'll be a lot of sex in my new life. There'll be a lot who won't want me, and a lot who will want me for the wrong reasons, freak show reasons. And I don't have the most active libido in the world. So these past few days may have to make up for a lot. And believe me, they will, they will.

I woke up very early this morning. Jake was still lying asleep, on top of the covers. I looked down at him. That thing between his legs. Once it had been the symbol of everything I hated about myself, everything that made me wrong, a freak, a stranger in my own body. Then for a glorious moment in time, it had been hard and straight and a connection of love between me and, quite probably, the only person who will ever understand me. Now it was nestled peacefully where it belonged, and I said an easy goodbye to it, with a tiny kiss, and a fond goodbye to its new owner. I tiptoed out early this morning, and caught the boat train. I left a note on Jake's pillow. It said: I'll always love you, you old bear, and good luck in America. That's where you're going, whether you know it yet or not.

Your pal and partner in crime,
Christine

14½ MacDougal Street
New York

May 19, 1953

Dearest Nick,

I wouldn't have believed it was possible for a man to be so open and honest and vulnerable. Certainly not in Winnetka, and you know something? Not in New York, either. Men are the same all over. Except for one. One wonderful man, and it's too wonderful to be true that he cares about me.

I'm not a jazz singer. Not yet. But Jerry Wexler thinks I can be, with about three years of very very hard work, and practice, and study, and a lot of singing. He says I can find the practice and study in New York, but it's a hard town to do an apprenticeship in. He's given me a letter of introduction to a great singer and teacher named Blossom Dearie, in ... Paris!

I can move to Paris and study and sing. And I'm sure I can find a cheap place to live. I met this friend of Jackie's who's working in the theater business, who just came back from studying at the Sorbonne, and she's told me all about the cafés and museums and sitting by the Seine, eating her lunch of bread and cheese and ... if she felt especially rich some days ... a tomato. It all sounds wonderful. I can get a small place and ... unless ... Oh, Nick, write me back and tell me if you want me to come!

Love,
Ronnie

Rue Catinat, Saigon

May 19, 1953

Dear Dad,

Long time no write.

I'd like to introduce myself. I feel like I've been through about a dozen lifetimes since we last saw each other. And now I see this column you wrote in the Paris Trib, and I can't believe you're the same man I fought with so much before I left home. We'll have a lot to talk about when next we meet.

I'm in Saigon. I can't tell you much more than that, except to say I'm attached to the Embassy in an advisory capacity. So, in a way I'm sort of working for your old firm, right? And you're a writer, and living in Paris. I guess we've kind of come full circle, haven't we?

I've become good friends with Fowler. You met him in Paris. He's a good guy, a bit cynical and unengaged, but that's the problem with all these old European types. The more I travel and the more I read, the more I've come to realize that in this world you've got to choose sides.

I've been reading a lot of York Harding lately. (He's actually my friend Larry

Darrell, writing under a pseudonym.) Do you know his books? The Role of the West, really interesting, really profound. And some articles in Encounter.

Anyway, I think I can do some good here, in a quiet way. The French have made a thorough botch of things, but Vietnam can't be allowed to fall to the Communists either. I've got an idea that a Third Force can be created that will act as an indigenous insurgency against both of them, and pave the way for the establishment of a truly free democracy in Southeast Asia.

I've met a girl. That's complicated too. And it involves Fowler. But that's all for another time, when I see you.

Affectionately,

Alden

Edward R. Murrow
CBS News
New York

May 21, 1953

Dear Jake,

It's been a couple of years since I wrote asking you to join my team for this television adventure I've embarked on, See It Now. Your reaction at the time, as I recall, was, "I wish goddamned television had never been invented." Words, as you know, I have uttered myself. In fact I suspected at the time you were quoting me, in a not-so-subtle dig at this reporter's selling of himself on an altar of tubes, wires, and breakfast cereals.

You may not have noticed, over there in Europe, but the damned medium seems to be here to stay, and I believe it has the potential for significant importance as well as virtually unlimited triviality. I'm looking to shore up my team here at See It Now, and I'd like to have you on board, old friend. There is big game to be hunted, and this is an adventure you will not want to miss.

You've been in Europe long enough, my friend. My guess is, we're fed up with pretty much the same things, and the same people. Let's take them on together. The danger is in America. And danger was always something you had a nose for.

Warm Regards,

Ed

Jacqueline Susann
100 Central Park West
New York, NY

June 15, 1953

Dear Ronnie,

Well, sweetie, Paris is three thousand miles from Broadway, but as long as you're happy. If you see Coco Chanel, give her my best, and ask her if she still likes being pinched on the ... well, maybe not.

Just make sure that guy you're with does you right. You know how men are--they won't buy the cow when they can get milk through the fence.

And check out my new address--and the new stationery. I met a fella who fit all my requirements. He's older (think yuck), but I've talked him into separate bedrooms and ya know, you don't have to buy the bull to get ... well, you get the idea.

He's Jewish ... and is he ever Broadway. He's a super press agent, and he tells me if I stop popping those dolls and start writing about them, he can guarantee me a best seller.

Drop me a line one of these, days, kiddo.

Your old pal,

Jackie

Mrs. Nicholas Carraway
Paris, France

July 21, 1953

Dear Jackie,

Wondering what happened to me, girl? I want to thank you for the friendship you extended to a dumb kid from the Midwest, and for all your sisterly advice, although I'm afraid I didn't end up taking much of it. Forgive me? But it all worked out for the best.

Nick and I were married last Friday. Blossom Dearie, the American singer, was my maid of honor. Albert Camus, the French writer, was Nick's best man. He had wanted his friend Jake, but Jake couldn't leave his work--he's in the middle of a big project with Edward R. Murrow, a television documentary about Senator McCarthy. Not only that, he's become close friends with my old mentor, Jerry Wexler, and he's going to start producing some jazz artists for Atlantic Records. And as he wrote to Nick, "Right now, the only thing that would get me out of New York with a crowbar would be a trip to New Orleans or Kansas City or Memphis."

I'm studying with Miss Dearie, and singing nights in a little cabaret. I even got to be a backup singer on a record Miss Dearie made--"Lullabye of Birdland" in French!

Nick works on his novel every day. I'm more or less supporting us until he gets his advance from M. Girodias, although M. Renoir has paid him to option the movie rights for Gatsby le Magnifique. But I don't mind. It's so exciting to see how he glows with an inner fire after a day of writing.

And ... married life is wonderful. We've actually been ... you know, without benefit of clergy, since I arrived in Paris. You can do that over here.

The only thing ... just between us girls ... I mean, I don't have much to compare with, except whatsisname ... but down there, he's--you know, a little bit ... smallish? But that doesn't really matter, does it?

Love,
Ronnie

ACKNOWLEDGMENTS

If this section were to be done right, it would run to book length all by itself. There are so many people, so many sources, that help push a project like this along.

One of the first to nudge this book from the talking stage to the doing something about it stage was Jim Idema, a great newspaperman and a great friend. I mentioned the idea to him over lunch one day, and he wouldn't let it alone. "When are you going to write that story about Nick Carraway and Jake Barnes?" Jim lived long enough to read the first draft, and he loved it.

Agent and former publisher Don Lamm liked what he saw. He provided early encouragement, and great help and advice every step of the way.

Sue Manocha, Claudia Jessup, India and Alex Richards, Ted Brooks, and Jenny Hickey copy edited and proofread the manuscript. Peter Jones gave advice and guidance.

We had the incredible good fortune to find the exact right editor in Lilly Golden, who understood and supported everything we were trying to do.

Thanks to the art department at Skyhorse for coming up with a great design and listening to our suggestions.

And a special thanks to two guys named Scott and Ernest, even though they don't exist.